BLOTS

by. T. Kulp

ISBN: 978-1-956612-02-8 (Paperback)
ISBN: 978-1-956612-00-4 (Hardback)
ISBN: 978-1-956612-01-1 (eBook)

This novel is entirely a work of fiction. The names, characters and incidents portrayed in it are the work of the author's imagination. Any resemblance to actual persons, living or dead, events or localities is entirely coincidental.

T. Kulp asserts the moral right to be identified as the author of this work.

Second print edition 2022

Making Adventure Publishing
16944 York Rd, Suite 63
Monkton, MD 21111

To Maria.

Thank you.

The scariest monsters are the ones

that lurk within our souls.

attributed to
Edgar Allan Poe

Contents

FORWARD

When I was in kindergarten my mom and dad received a call. The teacher was concerned. She asked, prodding but careful, if anything interesting happened at our house last night. My parents said no and asked why. The teacher recounted the story I told my class, a tale of murder and mystery that occurred in my backyard complete with an appearance of Spiderman to save the day. My first tale of the macabre was told at the age of five.

A storyteller was born.

Stories have been central to my life. Now, I want to share my stories with you.

Why call this book Blots? Like Inkblots, Rorschach Inkblots. Ghost stories are like these ink blots as different people find different elements scary. Is the ghost scary? Is the setting? Is the situation which caused the haunting? What you see depends on who you are and your life experience.

Like ink blots, in these stories I hope you will see something. Maybe yourself in the characters or ghosts. Maybe the setting is familiar. Some of what you see is there in the story. Some is not. And some is what your mind makes you see. Don't worry, what you see will stay between us. I can keep a secret.

Tim Kulp

8/28/2021

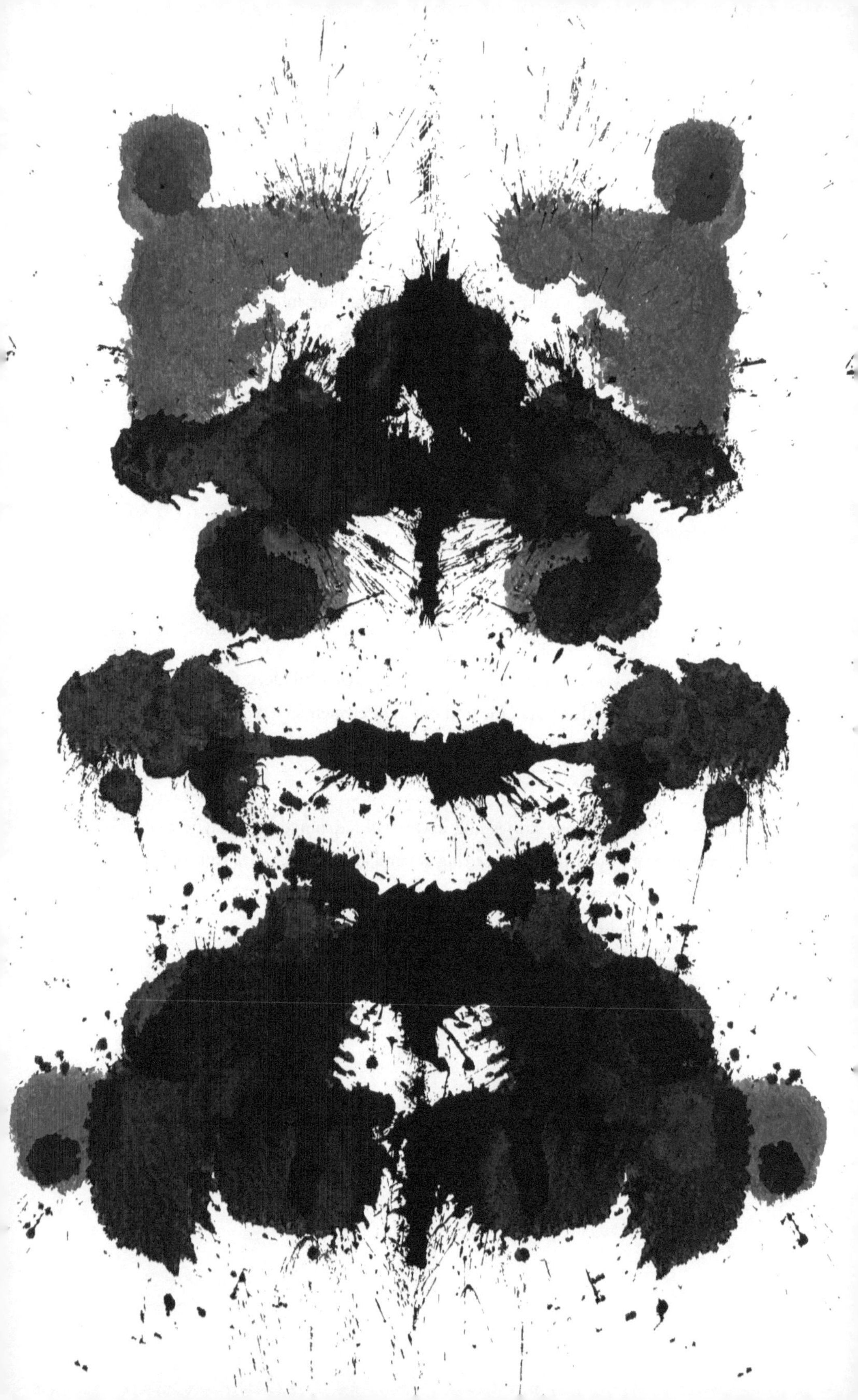

REFLECTIONS

The News

"So, like, I need glasses?"
I squint to see her face.
Is she joking?

"No, Mr. Paugh."
she huffs, annoyed.
Her fingers scratch over
the computer's keyboard
tapping out her diagnosis.

"You have a
very aggressive
posterior subcapsular cataracts.
Both eyes.
You're going blind…quickly."

Stabbing at the save button,
she turns to me,
huffs again
and stomps over to the sink.
Her heels slam against the tile floor.
Each clack piercing the headache
behind my eyes.

"Glasses aren't going to help
and your previous eye trauma,
from the accident,
makes surgery questionable
at best."

"So, what do I do?"
My brain jumps right to
"Yoga?"
then
"Essential oils?"
I chuckle at that.

                                        "No!"

She smacks the linoleum countertop.

                                "Listening when I said
                                wear protective eye gear
                                would have prevented all this.
                                But you didn't do that."

She moves to the sink
washing her hands.
I step closer
so I can see her
seeing me.

"Doc, I can't sculpt if I can't see."

My stomach gurgles
and instinct brings my hand
to my mouth.
But no need.
The nausea passes.

Her foot taps the rhythm of
irritable impatience.

What an inconvenience I must be.

How dare I
clog her morning routine
with such a distraction
as going blind.

"I've heard of
an experimental surgery…"
she balls up a paper towel
"it might be a possibility."
Throws the paper towel in the trash.

"Reality check.
Your eyes are in bad shape
from that car accident
a few years ago.
I told you to wear eye protection when you
work.
I told you this could happen.

You didn't listen."

She sighs at the weight
of dealing with me further.
"I'll see what I can find out
about the surgery.
I'll call you later in the week.

Wear eye protection Ed.
This can get worse."

"And lay off the alcohol.
Dehydration accelerates degeneration."
She sniffs the air with a grimace.

Walking out the door
she flips the colored tabs
marking the room available.

I stand in the examination room
listening to my thoughts
burst like pimples.

How will I work?

I've got so much left to do.
How will I get it done?

Oh Ed, you should have listened.

I'm an artist…
how can I create without seeing?

You didn't listen. Now you get what you deserve.

Glass isn't clay,
I need to see the glow,
feel the heat…

Alone and empty and nothing…that's what you deserve, Ed.

You reap
What you sow.

Being Seen

I walk out the exam room
into the showroom
where people are buying their
glasses.

Everywhere I look
mirror and glare and glow
scream into my eyes.

My stomach twists,
throat clenches
as I shield my face
and run for the door.

Going through the showroom
I hear the customers laugh.
They laugh with their faces in mirrors,
they laugh seeing themselves
with new glasses.

Everyone's happy with good news
and good moods.
Everyone sees their face in crisp clarity
while all I can see is muddy browns
and blurry edges.

No one else is going blind.
Just me.
Alone.

The only thing I can see almost clearly is
a woman and kid in the storefront window.
They're watching me.
She leans down
and whispers something into his ear.

He erupts in laughter.

She cackles
he chuckles
they laugh

at me.

They're a reflection in the window.

I turn to see them behind me
to tell the mom to fuck off.

I didn't get my eyes dilated.

I didn't get an eye exam.

I'm going blind.

I'm losing my art,
my work,
my life.

SO, STOP FUCKING LAUGHING!

I look behind me.

No one's there.

Looking back to the window
they're gone.

No woman.

No kid.

Just my reflection
staring back at me.

The Work

My warehouse studio,
my home,
is in the toxic waste section of town
where no one lives.

Surrounding me are
the decaying carcasses of old factories
forgotten when offshoring became a thing.

No one comes out here.
No prying eyes.
No leeches
pretending to care about me
while sucking away my creativity.

I can work in peace.

In my studio
my vision clears.
A momentary gift of crisp
clarity not to be wasted on
sunsets or people
but to see my sculptures.

I hurry to my current work: The Heart.

Six feet of sculpted glass almost complete.

My eyes drift to the walls
where glints of sunlight
flow through the heart and
paint the studio ruby red.

A deep red inspired by
an artist I met years ago
who mixed his paint with blood
to give it a smell the viewer would
fear.

Blood infused crimson arteries burst up
to the ceiling carrying my creativity
out into the world.

The purple veins snake
around my other sculptures
bringing their energy
into the heart.

My hand drags over the soft tubes
letting them lead me through my studio
as a lover's fingers trace his companion's spine in bed.

The veins take me to last year's project:
The Black Queen.

Made of black glass,
frozen,
glistening,
smoke
the Black Queen sits
on her throne
stretching five feet, six inches tall.

Her black dress drinks the light around her
in jagged ridges left sharp and ready
to cut any who embrace her.

I nod to the Queen
and continue.

My fingers dance
into the wisps of veins
now narrowing as they end
at the legs of Atlas.

My project from 3 years ago,
twelve feet tall,
emerald glass,
fading into blue at his waist.

The world he holds,
a silver mirror glass
showing the viewers
all they care about in the world.
Their own reflection.

People are selfish.

Oh Ed, you would know.

At dusk on the Equinox,
Atlas's mirror will catch the sunset
and throw it through the heart
turning this studio into a light show
until the horizon
swallows the sun.

The Equinox,
also known as opening night,
also known as three nights from now
when I welcome other artists
to see the heart.

When I return to the art scene.
Return from exile over a stupid
incident.

This time, I'll just drink enough
to be loose.
No arguments.
No fighting.

No

incidents.

The light show at dusk will be the
centerpiece of the night
and signal to everyone
I'm back. I'm ready
for them to see
my work.

For them
to welcome me
back.

So much to do.

This is going to be a shit show. You're a useless shit show.

The sharp edges of the furnace
melt into the blurry muddy gold
I've come to know with this blindness.

My moment of clarity is gone
but the work remains.
The deadline remains.

A glittering halo of sunlight pulls my eye to
a pile of glass on the workbench.
The pile meant for my next project,
a self-portrait.
I just need a vision for what it will be.
Who am I in glass?

I wonder
if I'll be able to see long enough
to start it.

Do you want to see you?
The real you?

The Encounter

I dump the red glass into my ceramic crucible
then dump the Coke into my glass of Jack Daniels.

Red is one of the few colors
I can see anymore.
Maybe that's why I chose the heart.
The world is muted and drab
but the boldness of red stays strong.
The world melts around me
but my heart stands out.

Yeah…that's good for my speech
on opening night.
Gotta remember that one.

Flicking the switches
I fire up the furnace.

Finishing my drink,
pouring the Jack & Coke into me
starts the last fire I need for tonight:
My creativity.

Instead of wood or charcoal,
this fire lights with whiskey and ice.

I'm out of ice.

Sweat makes my shirt into a second skin
telling me the melter is ready.
Stepping to the furnace
I pause to let the room
stop spinning.

Yeah Ed, drink to become who you wish you were.

Someone other than you.
Someone who can be something.

"Where's my blow pole?"
My eyes drift through the dancing shadows
and smokey darkness twisting
through the glass sculptures.
"There."

The Black Queen has it at her feet.
I smirk at her.
"Still want the pole, eh?"
Laughing.

You were empty and had nothing else to give her.
But you were a great taker. You took everything.
Parasite.

The glass is now a white glimmering pool
like dissolved magic in the furnace flames.
I stab the blow pole in
and swirl it like scooping honey.

A star comes out.
I roll it over my steel table.
Blowing a puff into it
the air presses the glass out
inflating
like a nova
before it bursts.

Now sculpting.

I stretch,
pull,
fold,
sweat
as the studio fades away
into the muted mud drenched darkness of night.
Only the cooling orange star
at the end of my tool
can be seen.

I refill my creativity.
Shaking out the last drops of Coke
leaving brown dots on the whiskey.
Islands of flavor in a sea of imagination.

My head sways.
The edges of a white dress catch my eye.

A woman stands at my window
watching me work
softly swaying in the night air.
A hypnotic sway
a siren's song of motion
pulling me towards her.

The wind sings to her
as blonde curls dance around her pallid face.

Dark red splotches
dribble down her chest
painting her white dress in
splashing waterfalls of...

Blood?
Did someone stab her?
Drop her off where no one would find her?

I step closer and see
the wind lifting her bangs
exposing frozen blue eyes fixed on me.
A smile slithers across her lips
as she slows her sway.

Another step closer,
and her transparency strikes me.
A reflection?
I spin to see her standing behind me
but no one is there.

Turning back to the window,
I notice her features are only highlights
with parts of her eaten by the night.
Ghostly outlines suggest her form,
a weightless phantom in the window.

"Get! Get out of here!
Private property!"

But she stays
swaying
watching with
amused eyes
and smirking lips
just like the woman at the eye doctor's office.

Another step closer,
stopping I see her now…

Now, I'm at the window.

"Amanda?"

She's not standing on the street.
She's floating
in the window.

"Are you a ghost?"
the words slip and slur from me.

My vision clears
bringing the world to full color and clarity
in time to see Amanda shake her head,
smile a predator's grin
and dissolve into the night with a faint
cackling laugh.

She's gone…

Putting my hand to the window,
I look into the night to see where she went
to see where she ran.

SMASH!

I spring back from the window
sobriety instantly crashing onto me
as I hear an explosion of glass.

Stumbling back
falling to the floor,
I push away from the window
from Amanda bursting through it

but the window is solid.

Spinning
I see the shattered remains
of tonight's work.

Thermal Stress

breaking the glass.

The window is whole
showing the empty night
a black void
with only the broken remains
of dead factories hinted by moonlit edges.

She's gone…

again.

The Hangover

Waking up I see the midday sun
pour glittering halos of light
through Amanda's window.

The white dress.
The same white dress she wore
at the wine festival.

The red blotches.
The blood was just
the wine I spilled on her
ruining that dress.

After that,
she only wore black.

Crawling off the mattress on my studio floor
my head pounds
making the blurs pulse further out of focus
throwing the world into
more muted
more muddy hues
with each throbbing beat.

By the furnace
last night's work lay in chips
and dust.

The sharp tangy smell of
shattered glass and failure drift
over the shards.

I didn't manage the temperature
and the last ventricle for my heart exploded.

Thermal Stress.

It cooled
too fast.

I left it on the workbench
too long.
Distracted by the window.

I get the broom
and pan
and sweep
and grumble.

"Accidents happen."

A shit show.

"Can't take my eyes off this work."

This shit show is no accident. It's who you are, Ed.
Another incident waiting to happen.

A slashing red X on my calendar
pulses out to me
marking the deadline for my heart.

Two more days.
Friday night,
opening night,
the Equinox only two days away.

I don't have time for these mistakes.
A year's work comes down to this Friday night.

AH!
Now it makes sense!
The idea steps into my mind
saying hello in exaggerated waves
like a comedian trying to get the audience to laugh.

It's been a year since Amanda left.
I was just thinking about her,
subconsciously,
and the Jack got me caught up
in the thoughts.

Shaking my head
dumping the broken glass
I chuckle at the ridiculousness.

Of course, I saw her in the dress.
That's the dress that ended things for us.
That dress is why she left
all worked up over an accident.

An incident.

The clock
is later than it should be.

11am on Wednesday.

I shut off the furnace
and throw on my jacket.
Lunch time Wednesday.
Time for drinks and dogs
at the Cadmium.

Drowning

Going down the wooden steps
of the Cadmium
is a descent into a cavern of drinks and depression.

The sun's painful glow disappears
behind a dark oak door.
The light of the world isn't for those
who come here.

Each step screams and squeaks under me
making me wonder:
When will one of these steps snap?
I'd fall through the broken steps
and be swallowed by this place.

Like so many before me.

Over the stairs creaking
and whining
I hear a familiar shout.
"Hey Eddy!"

I cringe at the name.
Eddy…
Ed is okay,
Edgar is fine.
Eddy is too childish.

My mom called me Eddy.
Only people who knew me
through her
call me Eddy.

My foot hits the tile floor
at the base of the steps
then peels off as I take another step.

Why is the floor always sticky here?

This is the first
and only time
I've been thankful for bad eyes.
It's saving me from seeing whatever
is on the floor.

Bernard taps away at the register
behind the bar.
"Eddy, you look like shit.
Need some hair of the dog?"

The dim bar lights glint off
Bernard's teeth
in bright white sparkles.
His dark brown skin and black clothes
are so blurry they make him
fade into the background of this place
with only those teeth
telling me where he is.

"Jeez Eddy, you squint any harder
and you going to bust a vein."

"Turn on a light around here
and I won't have to."
I snark
then plop down on my stool.

Back corner of the bar
near the elevator that never works.
Once it was a place
to see everything happening here
but now, I only see
muddy splotches of things,
maybe humans,
walking around, drinking, laughing.

Laughing at me squinting so hard?
No, probably not.

A Jack and Coke lands in front of me.
The sweet smell invites a sip as I lift it
and chuckle at the fizzing tickle
on my nose.

"Hotdogs?"
Bernard says.

"Yeah."
I groan through
the rumbling in my guts
not sure if it's hunger or
the least pleasant part of a
hangover.

"Seriously Ed, you look like shit.
Rough night?"
He leans in,
features getting clearer as he gets closer.
"You gotta get some food in you.
Hot sauce on those dogs.
Pep you up."

"Just seeing ghosts, I guess."
I laugh.
Bernard freezes and moves closer.

"Ghosts, huh?
My granny said the dead got lots to do,
so, if they come to see you,
you better listen."
He leans back away.

"Who you seein'?
Your mom?"

I shiver.
Shaking away the possibility.
Willing it to never be.

"Amanda, but she's not dead."
I take a soothing
burning gulp of Jack
there isn't much Coke in this drink.

Bernard slowly nods,
putting my order in the computer.
"Yeah, you fucked that all up."
The register beeps at him.

"Good lady,
chased away by your drunk ass."
He laughs.

"She was just pissed
I didn't want to change."
I clarify for Bernard.

"Nah, she was done with you
and all this."
He points to the drink
with a long fuzzy finger.

"You were the one saying you'd change.
I never heard her asking."

"She didn't have to say it."
I squinted harder to see if he was joking.
Can't see when people are joking
anymore.

"She just wanted something else.
Something I couldn't give."

Bernard's voice shifts from friendly
to parental.
"Ed, I've always told you straight.
That shit at the wine festival broke her
and she broke so bad, she ran away
cause no one
could put her back together."

"I spilled wine on her new dress?
What's so- "

"Your drunk stumbling
dropped a whole bottle
on her and when she got upset,
you told her she was stupid,
then, to complete your bullshit,
you told everyone to look at her
overreacting."

Bernard picks up a glass,
turning it in his hand
washing it with a sticky dirty rag.

The glasses here were real glass.
Heavy, durable, weighing something
when you filled them.
Weighing less when you emptied them.

You could feel your journey
from sobriety by
how heavy the glasses were
during the night.

By closing time
a full glass weighed less
than the first empty.
Each lighter,
empty glass begging to be filled,
to be something more than empty.
Something more than nothing.

"And everyone looked,
and they saw alright.
They saw your drunk ass being a dick."

"That's not what happened…"

Yes, it is.

Did my brain shut off before it got bad?
My mental recorder skipping
over the stuff
I didn't want to remember?

You deserve to see who you really are.

I finish the Jack and Coke,
and get up to go.
"This one on the house like usual
or is your shitty mood
gonna make me pay?"

Bernard clicks his tongue,
"Shitty mood? Ed,
I'm tired of watching you
killing yourself down here.
Just like your mom."

"Fuck that shit."
Snarling,
dropping my eyes
to the glittering
ice in my drink.

"Fuck that shit?
She'd sit down here drinkin' till
she couldn't get up those stairs.
What you doin'?

Sittin' on that stool.
You drink until you can't walk home.
Now you're seeing shit and I bet
you ain't done your project for
the opening yet.

You're sitting here drinking
when you should be home working.
Sounds like someone
we both know."

Disappointment drips from him
as my mouth gets hot,
saliva building up,
the herald of puking.

"What the fuck?
If I'm killing myself down here,
then why you giving me
Jack and Cokes?"

Hypocrite!

If I'm killing myself
then why does he keep putting
the gun in my hand?

He could stop the cycle.
Just keeps it going
like a multi-generational tab
that will come due when
I end up like
her
or
my dad.

He's not the one
seeing shit.
He's not the one
creating for the world.
He's just shoving guns in people's hands
and hoping for a tip.

"See, there, Ed…
you so use to drinkin' you can't tell.
That was just Coke.

That's why you don't pay.
I only give you Coke, no Jack for you,
not down here.

You so use to Jack and Coke, just a Coke
tastes like Jack to you."
He shakes his head
and grabs another glass.
"Go home. Sleep it off.
Finish your work.
Lay off the drink.

It's making you see shit
you shouldn't be seein'
and think shit
you shouldn't be thinkin'."

I shake off the words
as a chill strikes down my spine
stopping in my large intestines
rattling and quaking.
"Cancel the hotdog. I'm out."

Waving him away
I start up the stairs
hitting a run as my guts quiver again.
I'm going to explode…

The stairs scream and shout
as I stomp up them
forgetting their frailty.

Is it time?
Time for the stairs,
for this place,
to swallow me
like it swallowed
Mom?

Busting out the oak door
the light crushing down on me
burning my eyes.

I chant the prayer of drunkards stumbling home
in my mind...

Don't shit yourself.

Don't throw up.

Make it home.

Make it home.

My mobile phone rings
and I snatch it up
happy for the distraction.

"Hello?"

"Mr. Paugh, Ed,
this is Doctor Rickman,
your eye doctor."
She huffs, sick of me already.
"Looks like you're qualified
for the surgery
and insurance is going to cover it.
Can you come by Saturday?
It's quick, in and out the same day."

"Yeah, yeah I can do that."
The sickness is washed away.

"Do you have any family
that's coming with you?"
She asks.
"You will need a driver."

"No. I'll just
wait it out."
I say.
Thinking of family
bringing me back
to sickness.

"Great, we'll put you at 10.
Don't call to reschedule
at the last-minute Ed.
You need this."
She hangs up.

I smile.

I'll see again.

Hope

drowns

ghosts.

Skeletons

I couldn't work
so I sat out here to watch the sunset.

These lawn chairs
make a little porch
where I can look over the emptiness around me
and get my mind in the right place.

Bernard's wrong.

He doesn't understand the pressure of an artist.
People clamoring to see my creation,
judging my work,
judging me.

This is how I'll get found.
How I'll get somewhere other than here.
How I'll be someone worth something.

I didn't want to be an artist.
It found me.
It pulled me out of Dad's accident…
pulled me out the car
every night when I dreamt of those lights,
the rum on his breath,
the insanity in his cackling laughter
when the car
SMASHED
into us.

The golden sun dips below the factory carcasses
kissing their broken windows
and boarded-up doors
with the last of daylight.

I sip my Jack and Coke,
opening my mind for tonight's work
getting my creativity primed.

Mom was the Jack drinker.
She'd say, "Don't waste your time."
When she'd look at a drawing,
a painting,
a sculpture.

She was my worst critic.
"I'd be nothing.
It's genetic."
No…
critics simply judge your work
not your value as a person.

Mom wasn't a critic.
after all.

"You're just like your dad."
She'd scoff.
"He had dreams too. And now look at him.
Took all those medics to scrape him out that car."

Not my future. Not me.
I let the burn of Jack take me away
from thoughts of her.

When I found this place
I knew it'd be a great art studio.
A place where I could be free to create
without watching eyes
without judgment.

But you didn't find this place.

Crowley did.

Oh, that's right.
Crowley, good old, Crowley.
I take a deep drink,
cheering the man
who introduced me to
alcohol.

Swearing off alcohol
after Dad's crash
didn't last long
when Crowley was around.

I used to say no.
Not now.
Then he taught me to say:
Don't stop.

Haven't seen him
since he moved out of the studio,
guess that was three years ago now.

The stars start poking through dusk
and my mind is loose
ready
stretched for an evening of work.

Or staggering, stumbling drunk.

No! Stretched and ready.

Going inside,
I leave my chairs outside.
No one comes around here.
This place is a graveyard
for businesses,
for work
and people hate graveyards.

They fear that some of the death
found here
might cling on to them.

Follow them home,
an infection
leading to
their decaying
rot.

My work needs to get done.
Two days…
The Equinox,
the opening
comes in two days.

Starts

As night comes on
my head swims in the seas of creativity.
I fire up the furnace.

Loading the red glass
into the crucible,
warming the blow pole,
bringing my tools to the table
including a fresh full glass of whiskey.
I'm already out of Coke I bought today?
I'll get more again tomorrow.

Swirling the white molten glass
on the blow pole
the studio fades into the mud
that now drowns my world.

A white-hot star
exploding with each puff of air
expanding with each swirl in the glowing honey.

Sweat drips onto the floor
as I take another drink
to keep my creative fires stoked.

I stretch and shape
and fold and form
sculpting the star on my pole
into the last ventricle
of my heart.

DONG!

My clock strikes midnight.
A rusty,
menacing tone
hangs in the studio
silencing the furnace's roar and
my panting breath.

A quiet tapping,
quiet rapping
at my window
cracks the silence.

"Finish this cause you're out of time.

Gotta get this into the annealer tonight.
Gotta attach it tomorrow."

Look at the window.

"Focus!"

Look

at

the

window…

Slamming my eyes shut,
I open them to brilliant clarity.
The world returns to its true hues
and crisp lines.

The windo-

"Shut up!"
I rush over to the annealer,
open it
and gently place the ventricle inside
to start the cooling process
to avoid

Thermal Stress.

I mop my forehead
busting the sweaty surface
exploding the
stinging salty water over my face.

Look at the window.

"No!"
I drink again
feeling the burning Jack catch in my throat
deciding if it is going down
or coming back up.

Vomit slushes through my teeth.
I catch it before it dribbles out.
Swallowing a quick cough
I wash down the puke
with a long drag of whiskey.

Pressing my hand across my mouth
to keep everything in
my eyes drift to the window.

A man sits in my lawn chair.
He is looking at the factories.

I move closer to see him.

He slowly turns
his spine popping and shifting
with each degree of rotation
like a rusty watch being
wound to the hour.

He's facing me now,
eyes drenched in disgust
watching me sway
as my legs go unsteady
unable to hold the weight of
recognition.

Crowley.

Good
old
Crowley
sitting in my lawn chair
watching me work.

My eyes drop to the empty whiskey glass
and I nod.
"Seeing things."
I snort a laugh
and return to the furnace.

Amanda's voice rings in my head,
no, not my head,
from across the room.

From the window beside Crowley.

"Oh, Ed…"
a spite-soaked cackle ripples around me.
"You're not imagining this."

I turn back,
seeing her white dress,
red blotches,
swaying.

Crowley now stands beside her
in his white shirt, paint-stained pants
with two paint brushes dangling
from his pockets.

His palette of choice for
the Irish landscapes he paints:
vivid green
and bright blue.

"Ed, we're here to see the shit show."
Crowley snarls in a gleeful tone.
His face curls around those
snaggle teeth
in a shit eating grin.

"You were always good for a shit show."
He shakes his head.
"Not much else."

"You're both hallucinations
from dehydration and stress."
I wave them away.
"I'm going to pass out now."
I drop on the couch.

"Sure, we could be…"
Crowley says.
"but we're not.
We're here to see you do to yourself
what you did to us."

Amanda's eyebrows pop up
and she nods with a mischievous smile.

She hisses,
"You're a vampire Ed.
You suck the life out of everyone.
Sure, they feel good while you do it
but when you're done
they're left drained and broken
and wondering what happened."

I sit up to see them.
"A vampire?
I don't remember you complaining
Amanda.
The parties and art openings
and people fawning over you.
Yeah, real hard life."

"Ed, sweetie, you don't remember
because you were always drunk."
She sways her hypnotic sway
making me want her,
want to touch her,
if I weren't spinning on the couch
I'd go to her.

"Everything was about you
and I thought I could help,
but in the end, you didn't want help.
You wanted an excuse.
You drank because of me.
Remember saying that?

I made it impossible to work.
Remember saying that?"

Yes.

"That's not what happened."
I correct her.

"And what's your problem Crowley?
You got famous at my shows.
Now you live
in New York with that model
in a mansion.
Yeah, I was so horrible."

"Ha! Your shows?
Those were our shows Ed."
Crowley rubs his long red beard.

Stroking the twisted curls
like a bad actor
preparing for a flashback scene.
"In fact, I paid for those shows.
You didn't have a dime.
I paid for the shows and
you told everyone
they were your shows
and I was a…what did you say…

oh, yes, an artist
trying to keep up
with
you."

Crowley stands.
His features drift in and out
of the night's darkness.

"You sold more work than I did.
But I was always dragging you
to our shows.
Getting you sober enough
to make an appearance.
I wasn't chasing you down, Ed.
I was holding you up."

He laughs again.
"Yeah, I gave you everything.
Every penny I had
trying to save you.
You left me with nothing.
No one would come to my shows
because they were afraid
you'd be there, drunk off your ass.

After you got into that fight,
your drunk idiot self
punched that guy
no one would show up to our shows.

I moved to New York
because I had to go somewhere
no one knew you.
So I left everything.

My parents.

My friends.

My life here
just to start fresh.

To start a life without you."

Parasite.

Vampire.

You suck the life out of someone.

You leave a disease behind.

The disease of distrust and doubt.

"Whatever Crowley! That's all shit!"
The crisp edges give way to
wet smudges
dissolving to blurs
as a third face starts to appear
behind Amanda.

A small face.

Further away
approaching slowly.

I squint
seeing a distant sad stare
in that face.

The room spins faster.
I fall back on the couch.
Sliding off to the floor.

"See you tomorrow Eddy boy!"
Crowley growls a trailing belly laugh.

Amanda joins in with a cold echoing
cackle.

Cold as the floor.
The cold comfortable floor…

Sleep.

Guests

"Good morning, Eddy boy!"
I spring up to Crowley's voice.

"What?
What time is it?
Did I miss the show?"
The morning light presses through
my heavy eyelids.

Crowley always wakes me up like this.

Loud, immediate,
at least he didn't flip me out the bed
this time.

"No, that's tomorrow night."
He says.

I open my eyes
finding my studio
not our old apartment.

No Crowley,
just me.

"Must have-"

"Nope, you're not dreaming."
Crowley shouts
waving at me from the window.
Amanda is there too, cackling a laugh.
Both of them looking too chipper
for this early.
"We're really here."
he says.

I rub my eyes again
the world now a deeper mud
colorless except for
the dead gold hues
and bright halos that engulf everything
in blinding sunshine.

Hallucinations
with a hang over?
That's what's happening here.
I get up to make coffee.
I'm out of coffee.
Opening the refrigerator,
finding nothing
but the last mouthfuls of Jack Daniels.

"That's the breakfast you're looking for."
Amanda shouts
pointing to the bottle.

I look at her stupid giddy face,
those excited flapping curls,
that erotic sway,
that bloody white dress.

She's clear.

Crowley's clear.

Everything else is blurry and muted.

Yep, hallucinations.
If they were real, they'd be blurry too.

I can barely see
the windows from here.

"Fine, I'll play along."
I snap up the bottle and finish it.
"Happy?"

"Not since I met you babe."
Amanda says with a spiteful grin.

Tomorrow's the day.
No time to waste.
I get to work.
Pulling the ventricle
from the annealer.

It's perfect.

The form is right
but the details are too muted,
too colorless to see
so I brush my fingertips over it
drinking in the smooth, soft feel.

As I work
the two of them
keep shouting
and laughing
and second guessing
and pointing out problems
and saying all the things that usually
don't come out of my mouth.

"You aren't as good as you think."
Crowley says.

"You think people will like
that?"
Amanda says
launching into a rippling cackle.

"Your work's really gone
down the drain…
or down the bottle."
Crowley says
with a self-satisfied chuckle.

But the laughing,
God their laughing!
I'd take the hot dollop of glass
to my ears if it would help.

But it won't.

Their laughing
is just like my dad's
before the crash.
Maniacal.
Engulfing.

I hear him
in them.

Hallucinations
playing off
trauma.

They are hallucinations.

And hallucinations don't
scream in your ears.
"Shut up! Stop laughing!"

But they don't.

                              "If you would have listened
                              to Dr. Rickman, you'd see how bad
                              this is."
                              Amanda snipes
                              then cackles that goddamn rattling cackle.

                              "Yeah, you should have listened to her."
                              Crowley barks a laugh.
                              "She'd have saved your vision and
                              the embarrassment of showing this shit."

The sun starts to droop
to the factories in the distance.
Flashes of sunset pierce
the windows that aren't boarded up.

The boards!

That's it.
"Last chance you two.
Shut up or I'll shut you up!"

They laugh in unison
with Amanda's cackle drowning Crowley.

The heart rattles
like the singing of a hell spawn chorus
where every note and beat
begs me to end everything
to escape it.

"Have it your way!"
Grabbing my crowbar
and hammer
I storm out the studio.

Silent and Voiceless

Smiling
I kick open the studio door.

Amanda and Crowley
talk among themselves as I come in
tossing down sheets of plywood.

"Got this from the factories for you two."

I stomp to Crowley's window
slapping on the plywood
hammering it to the windowsill.

"That won't work."
Crowley calls out.
"You'll still hear us."

He's not even muffled…

Damn.

He's right.
I can hear him
and not just in my head.
I can hear him
in the room with me.

Just like I hear Amanda's amused snickering
as she turns and points to my failing.

"Fine!"
I rip off the plywood
throwing it across the studio.
It slides to a stop near the heart
missing the veins on the way.

No cracking,
no ting of fracture,
no pop of explosion,
just the laughing.

That

damn

cackling

laughing.

She never laughed like that
when we were together.
That isn't her in the window.

That's a hallucination!

Crowley belly laughs
pointing
at me failing.

"You idiot Ed. You can't keep us quiet."
Crowley says through the laughter
choking as spittle hits the window.
"We're here until the end.
Until you do to yourself
what you did to us."

Their laughing
matches the throbbing in my head
like I'm rolling in a tumbler
of their derision
each fall smashing into my face
splitting my skull…

Smashing?

Grabbing the crowbar
I rush to Crowley
and throw the cold steel through his face.
His laughing silenced by the explosion of glass
blowing out of the studio into the brown blob of grass
and colorless mud painted night.

Screams overtake Amanda's laughing
her face gaping in shock
and terror
as I come for her next
silencing her with a shatter
busting the window into the night.

Now I laugh.

Loud.

Hearty.

Soul cleansing laughter.

Choked short by the appearance of a third ghostly face.
Another face. In another window.
The boy.

The boy that was with Amanda in the glasses store.

But…

I don't know him?

"Who are you?"

"I'm Allister.
I don't expect you to remember me."
He says quietly
as his image becomes clear
sharp and colorful.

A pale boy,
dark eyes,
dirty hair,
worn,
torn clothes.

"I was in your art class."

I don't remember him
but the class,
that comes crashing into me
popping and snapping like the accident.

"Mr. Paugh, you were amazing.
Your art was so wonderful
and you made me believe
maybe I could be an artist too."

A faint smile drifts over the boy.
"You said,
art isn't about talent,
it's about

vision

and anyone can have

vision.

I thought I could have vision.
I didn't have talent, but I could have

vision."

The boy perks up,
his chest popping out
"I wanted to be like you.
And when my dad would tell me
I wouldn't be anything
I just remembered what you said."

His chest collapses.
The night sky deepens his reflection
leaving him a phantom of an outline.

"Dad would come home
and tell me
I couldn't be anything
cause he wasn't anything
and people like us can't be anything.

And I knew he was wrong
because you said
all I need is

vision.

Then I found out,
you were teaching our class because
you had to.

You had community service
from your car accident,
from being drunk and driving
and hitting that lady.

Drunk just like my dad.
He was always drunk too."

Somber tones devour his frail voice.
"My dad was right
and you proved it.
People like him,
people like me,
people like you
can't be anything.

Too busy drinking to do anything else."

Allister watches
the words impact me.
A collision but no accident,
it's an intentional strike of malice.

The boy sinks into the lawn chair
behind him.
"That's not true!"
I strangle the crowbar
preparing another swing
this one in disgust
not at the boy
but at his

truth.

"You're alone Edgar Paugh.
You're talented,
you have

vision,

and that's it.

You've drank away
everything else,
everyone else
and now stand alone
in your empty glass studio."
The boy smiles now showing
a mouth full of fangs and venom.

"Just like my dad.

You have nothing.

You are nothing."

The deadliest venom.

Truth.

"I'm not nothing!"
Swinging the crowbar
bashing the kid
into a rain of shards.

The shards slash and slice through me
as I fall into the colorless grass
into a pool of glass.
"I'm not nothing!"

Silence

"I'M NOT NOTHING!"

In the cold almost fall night
I look back into my studio.
The calendar calls me.
The red X glowing on Friday,
tomorrow,
the Equinox.

I'm not nothing.
I'm an artist.
I have

vision.

But glass is all over my lawn.
Now in my palms,
in my knees and elbows
sticking out like claws
ready to snag another chunk of me.

Firing up the furnace,
I pick up each piece of glass,
each bit of the three windows
pulled from the grass,
plucked from my skin
and drop the shards into my crucible
with a faint clink.

This is the last crucible
for my heart.

I toss the glass into the melter.

I prep my tools.

One last addition to the heart.
A final prison for
Crowley,

Allister

and Amanda

so, I can be done with them.

I'm not who they say I am.

Yes, you are Ed.

You can't smash who you are.

I'm not who they say I am.
I'm not nothing.

The Opening

"No thank you."
I wave away the drink tray
and drain another gulp
from my water bottle.

Sitting on the couch,
I hear the crowd circulating
around the heart
commenting on the craftsmanship,
the bold colors,
the exquisite forms.

I smile
at the satisfaction that they see me.

My talent.

My abilities.

That
I'm full
of potential.

"Damn Eddy,
you got a good turnout here."
Bernard's familiar voice whispers
as I feel the wave of the couch
from him crashing down beside me.

"Are the glasses just for the look or
is it that bad?"

"It's that bad."
I nod
forcing a smile.
"I can't see anything after last night."

Remembering for a moment
the last thing I saw,
the pouring of the molten glass
into the heart,
then listening all night
soberly sitting and listening
for any cracking, any fracture
or frailty to destroy my masterpiece.

The muddy browns turned black
after the pour
and I sat to see the sunrise
but instead, only heard the alarm clock.

DING!

The bright ding of crystalline delight,
a fairy tale ding like those
that awoke Scrooge.

Blind
but quiet.

Alone
but hopeful.

"I'm glad to see you,
like this,
tonight."
Bernard breathes deep.
"You've done good here."

Bernard pats my shoulder.
"I think you'll be back on the art scene
with all this attention.
I wish your…"
He trails off
holding the silence between us.
"…well, you should be proud of what
you've done here.
I'm sure other people would be."
He stands quietly.

"Welp, off to see if
I can convince some rich lady
to make me her boy-toy."
He pats my leg
and I smile
a real smile
finding joy in the darkness.

DING!

My clock chimes, five till sunset.
It's time.

I step to the front of the heart
wading through waves
of thunderous applause.

Raising my hands
their energy,
their love
fills me.

"Thank you all for coming."
Silence falls over them.
"This sculpture has been a journey.
And I hope tonight,
you take that journey with me."

"This is my heart,
my creativity,
that I want to share with the world.
The veins pull in my past,
the arteries,"
I point to the ceiling
"send my energy to the world.
To all of you in hopes that you
feel the power to create something
of your own."

Thunderous applause erupts
and I hear the glass heart singing behind me
echoing their adoration
in a rattling song
and…
is that laughing…
no, singing.

"Mr. Paugh,
we've been wondering all night…"
a woman says
"Who is the family in the heart?"

Grinning,
I think about how everyone sees
themselves in art.

There isn't a family in the heart
only the perfect glass form
of a human circulatory system
meant to pump my genius
into the world
as lifeblood
to other artists.

"Ma'am who do you think they are?"
I ask
indulging her question.

"I don't know…your parents maybe?
From when you were a child?"
She asks.

"A man, a woman and a child
all laughing.
I'm guessing you had
a happy childhood."

Everyone laughs or giggles
including me.
I push away the grimace
before anyone sees it.

My nose fills with
the hot breath of
Rum and Whiskey.

"I didn't put a family in the heart."
I chuckle and shake my head.

"Oh, did you have a collaborator?
Did they put the family there?"
She asks.

Confusion starts
rippling over the audience
and resonating in my gut.

The heart sings again,
no, not singing,
laughing.

Insane
cackling
laughter.

I turn to see the sun falling
to the angle I projected,
Atlas's mirror catching the beam of light
and throwing it through
the crimson heart
exploding red through the studio.

Beams of light
blasting into my eyes
rushing towards me before the crash.

But I don't see the red.
I only see the three faces in my heart…

Crowley,

Amanda,

and Allister.

All staring at me
faces twisting in horrid laughter
exaggerated and stretched by contempt.

The masterpiece isn't singing
or rattling
it's laughing.

The studio is baptized in my heart's
bloody fire.

The faces laugh.

The people ooh and ahh and cheer and laugh.

They're all laughing.
Everyone is laughing.
My heart is laughing at me.
My masterpiece is laughing at me.

Laughing that I didn't know
someone fucked with it.

Squeezing my fist
the cold steel of the crowbar
is there.

Did I pick it up?

Was it always there?

Red is all I see
replacing the muddy muted hues
with a world of fire and blood.

"Stop laughing!"
I swing.

SMASH!

Screams

"Stop laughing!"

Swinging

SMASH!

Screams and shouts
and cries are drowned in
their laughter.
Crowley's belly laughing.
Allister's childish giggles.
Amanda's hellish cackling
that I can't stop hearing no matter how loud I scream.

SMASH!

Swinging again
and again
the air now red dust
and stabbing pain.

"Stop laughing!"

But she doesn't
and the kid and Crowley
and the screams fade
leaving only laughing
as I run to the Black Queen

SMASH!

And run to Atlas

SMASH!

And run to the pile of glass
the pile that would be me
and I hate it
every plate of it
a disgusting heap of shit
that deserves this

SMASH!

the veins

SMASH!

the arteries

SMASH!

the bottles

and glasses

and tools

and shelves.

SMASH!

SMASH!

SMASH!

The laughing

stops.

Everyone is gone.

Everything is silent.

The sun falls under the factories
and I'm alone.
The red turns to blackness
as my vision dissolves into blurs
fading further
now only the empty void

and I fall

sliding down the wall

hitting the floor.

Alone.

Empty.

Nothing.

Surgery

White gauze
is a welcome change to the
infinite blackness I've had
since last night.

Dr. Rickman unwraps my head
and the lights show their glow
fading into a bright neon lit room.

"There we go Mr. Paugh."
Rickman pulls the last bandage off.
"How's that look?"
Her voice is caring and curious.

"I can see."

The world once again has sharp edges
and crisp lines
and an endless palate of colors.

"I can see!"

"Yeah, surgery went great."
Rickman says with a smile.
"We use this new surgical glass to
reinforce your eye.

It also works as a lens
to correct your vision.
You're probably seeing better
than you ever have."

Tears burn in the corner of my eye.

"What's wrong Mr. Paugh?
Are you experiencing any pain?"
Rickman asks with the care
of a good mother.

"No, I just…"
choking
"This week has been horrible,
and I feel like I've lost everything.

Now I can see again.
And maybe, start again."

The waterworks come on now
as the tears drizzle off my nose and splotch in clear puddles
on the surgery gown.

"Well Mr. Paugh,
have you heard the expression:"
She leans close to me.
"When you've lost everything,
you're free to become anything."

A quick pat on the shoulder,
a bright smile
and Dr. Rickman steps out of the room
telling the nurse to check on me
in a few minutes.

She's right.

I've lost everything.

My art is destroyed.

My studio ruined.

My career shattered.

I have nothing.

Now, I can be anything.

"Oh, no you can't Ed."
a soft voice whispers beside me.

"You can only be Edgar Paugh,
the piece of shit."
her voice trails into a cackle,
Amanda's cackle.

I tense
and look
seeing her white dress float out
from beside me.

"Yeah Ed, you're still a piece of shit.
Smashing all that stuff
didn't change who you are."
Crowley belly laughs,
stepping into the room
from the corner of my eye.
"You can't smash who you are."

"I smashed you!"
Shaking my head
trying to rattle them loose.

"You're all broken!"

"Nah, we're still here."
Allister says with a grin
crawling onto a chair.

I slam my eyes shut
to escape
but they're still there.

They're in the dark behind my eyes.

Opening them again,
they're still there in the room's light.

"You tried to get rid of us Ed."
Amanda whispers into my ear.
Her seductive tone
tightens every muscle in me
pushing out a whimper.
"But, you can't get rid of us now."

"Yeah, Ed. We're in your head now."
Allister points to his eyes.
"Surgical glass."
He points to my eyes.

"That's right Ed.
We're like a family now."
Amanda whispers again.
"You'll always have us."
She leans in.

Her breath tracing over my ear
sucking the warmth from my soul
as she breathes in.

"And we'll always have you."

Author's Note:

Reflections

2020 - 2021

I wrote Reflections in a weekend with most of it being delivered in a feverish frenzied Friday night. After the original draft, I rewrote the story numerous times and explored the different characters that showed up.

Edgar's parents were a late addition to the story. In the last draft of the story, I was wondering why Edgar is the way he is. Why does he obsess about his art and drown himself in whiskey? Exploring the idea, I landed on Edgar's real desire in this story is to be loved and accepted. He doesn't know how to give those things because he didn't have models to show him how. The curse of our upbringing is a common theme in my stories. We are who we are shaped to be and often, shape others through our behaviors. My own behaviors and their impact on my kids is on my mind with this story.

The story came from a writing prompt requesting a story about an artist. My wife and I were kicking around the concept and she told me about how glass blowers wear eye protection because of the infrared light emitted by the ultra-heated glass. A bit of research later and I found out that is totally a thing. Without the eye protection, the glass blower's eyes burn out from the light of the hot glass (simplifying here). The seed of the story was born.

I enjoyed the glass imagery throughout the story and found unintended parallels showing up during my writing. While I didn't set out to make the glass such a core feature of the story, it really showed up. Now, as I re-read the story, I am enjoying all the symbols and metaphors that are created with the glass.

You might notice a few things that appear in this story referencing one of my favorite authors: Edgar Allan Poe. A few references here are the Tell-Tale heart (the heart sculpture), the Bells (referenced in the clock chimes) and other of his works are strewn about. Also, it is no accident that the main character is named: Edgar. I love Poe's ghost stories that leave the reader wondering if it was really a ghost or just the guilt of the main character. Do you think Amanda, Crowley and Allister are ghosts or guilt?

THE WISP

I scream up the cliffs. Seeing the swaying rope above me, feeling the rest of the rope around my waist. Screaming again.

With the waves and distance and revelry of the festival…no one will hear me up there. No one will know, the rope broke and I'm not hanging there anymore. The sun plunges towards the ocean. I don't have much time to get back up there.

Climbing over crags, heading towards the road to the cliffs, a boy catches my eye. His muddy threadbare clothes drape over his skeletal body. Long soaking black hair breaks around his dirty face revealing eyes grayer than a stormy sea.

"Hey! Get out of here!" I shout to him.

He turns and runs towards town, towards the road to the cliffs. I scramble over the rocks, rushing to catch him.

"Hey kid! You can't be here today!"

The boy silently runs just out of reach. I swipe to catch him, but he sprints ahead, passing the fishing boats, passing my dad's boat, the one that became my boat.

"Fishing is how this town lives Theo. Ain't no time for adventurin'." My dad's voice stops me.

I snap around to see a 10-year-old me listening as he hefts nets and chum boxes around the deck. The stink of mince fish floats around me drowning the sea's salty fresh freedom.

(THEN)

"If I had this boat," I point to the horizon, "I'd sail until I found where the sun comes from. So far, I'd see different stars at night." My words are a cocktail of hope and possibility, intoxicating me with what could be.

"You can't do that Theo!" 10-year-old Kyle gasps, scandalized by the blasphemous words. "My pa says we gotta be here for the festival. Everyone's got to be here!"

"Nah!" I shake off the idea and squeeze his arm, pressing my confidence into him. "You can come with me Kyle!" Whispering and leaning closer to him. "We'll be like those books people bring to town! Those adventures we found. Two friends against the sea."

Kyle rips away from me vigorously shaking his head to drive away the thought.

"Well Theo, when you ain't got bills or family or any responsibility…" Dad's eyes dig into mine. Making sure I understood, "you do that. Take this boat, go that way. Festival will be fine without ya." He laughs.

When he died, I started fishing with his boat. When mom died, I kept fishing with his boat, never leaving the bay. I was a fisherman like my dad. Who else could I be? With no anchors into this town, I'd float adrift. I was a fisherman. What else could I be?

(NOW)

The streetlamps flicker on snapping me back to now. The first frozen breath of night blows in from the horizon. I've got to get to the cliffs. The boy catches my eye as he rounds the street corner.

"Boy! It ain't safe here tonight!" He doesn't stop, doesn't slow, just goes faster.

Following him, seeing the boy stutter step. He scans the road to the cliffs and then looks down an alleyway. As I reach him, he dashes into the alley disappearing through a tight staircase.

I can't follow. No time. Gotta get to the cliffs, to the festival. Looking into the alley, I turn away

"You're on your own k- "

The sight of the Cork Tavern steals my thoughts from him. The yellow building, the red metal barrel sitting outside those wooden doors concealing a dimly lit black bar where I met-

(THEN)

"Funeral?" she straddles the bar stool beside 23-year-old me. I shake my head keeping my eyes on my water. Across the bar, her friends whisper and nervously giggle probably scared that she was talking to a local. College girls were always wary of us locals…and I don't blame them. But she's fearless. Her posture and radiance and grace would break the worse storm at sea. I have no choice but to shrink into my stool. "I saw you sitting here alone, looking all sad and thought you might be coming from a funeral."

I smirk, not daring to look at her auburn curls or glowing hazel eyes this close.

"No ma'am." My voice crackles under the disbelief welling in my throat. "Just thinking about something my dad said."

On the edge of my vision, I see her lean closer. An intoxicating smell of jasmine and whiskey drift from her. Finding a shadow of courage in me, my eyes sneak to hers. Deep, bright light brown suns for eyes, curious, hungry, and looking for adventure.

"I'm Jay from Dublin. Well, actually I'm from Ohio in the States but I'm staying on campus in Dublin."

Taking my eyes back to my water, "Hi…I'm Theo. I…fish." A slight smile flicks across my face as I shuffle away from her on my stool. Why is she talking to me? When will it start? When will her friends start pointing and laughing and everyone see how stupid I am to think someone like her would talk to something like me…? But they don't.

"Theo, you look like someone I use to know. He had a hard night too. But…I didn't notice how hard his night was when I should have." She forces a grin through mounting tears, shakes her head and taps the bar. Like a summoning spell the bar tender appears and pours her a whiskey. "Can I get you a drink?"

"I uh…I, don't drink alcohol." I turn away. Her hand grabs mine, a warm grasp asking my eyes to meet hers. She snickers and smiles.

"Theo the fisherman…how about I get you a water?"

And she does. And we talk. And she is amazing and interested…interested in me. Hours pass as we laugh, and I tell her about my boat, my dad's boat, the bay, and the fish. She tells me about her school and family back home and her future as a writer. Her stories are filled with fantastic places like Beavercreek, Ohio, and fantastic ideas like traveling so far that you can't go back home for days. She flew to the horizon to find where the sun came from and instead found me. We talk about her brother, he had the rough night that ended in suicide. She cries, I hold her hand. I tell her about my dad's advice to leave but how I'd just be adrift if I did. We talk about loss and prisons and decisions that led us here to this moment.

I guess these things are easier between strangers. You can talk about mistakes and anxiety, inadequacies and failures. No fear of judgement because the stranger will be gone in a moment and never think of you again.

She straightens on her stool, her perfect teeth breaking through an angelic smile.

"We're heading back to Dublin on the next train." She nods to her friends. "Come with me. Who knows what awaits Theo the fisherman in the big city?" She springs up and away towards the bathroom. "I'll be right back."

23-year-old Kyle jumps into her seat. "Whoa Theo! Did she just ask you to go into the city?"

"Uh, yeah. She did." I chuckle shaking away the absurdity of the situation.

"You goin'?" Kyle pushes into my view. His face excited and surprised. An idea bursts through his drunken fog. "Wait…do you think she's a Wisp? Trying to trick you to leave the village? Trying to get you to break the pact?" His face coiled with uncertainty.

I scoff so hard my throat scruffs like sandpaper.

"We gotta miss the festival to break the pact and that ain't for another few years. She's no Wisp. She's not some monster trying to pull me away just a drunk city girl making a joke." I shake my head to bring reality back, to burst this dream of someone like Jay being interested in me. Of me leaving here. Of me being someone…else.

"She's coming back. I want to hear everything tomorrow." Kyle whispers while trying to sneak away unnoticed.

"So?" Jay asks as her friends pack up.

"Thanks Jay but I'm not really a city person." The words jump out of me like she threw snakes on my lap. All the reasons why I shouldn't go keep gurgling into my mind with all the worse things that could happen screaming so loud I can't hear anything else. I can't hear the question I should have been asking: What is the best thing that could happen? Escape? A new life? A new me? All these possibilities drowning in the nervous stomach acid of doubt and fear.

Jay shrinks from me, disappointed, nodding, tossing me a feigned smile then leaving with her friends. I keep my eyes to my water, but my mind follows her out the door, follows her into a night of escape, a night of being anyone, a chance to be more than a fisherman stuck in this town.

She left her whiskey.

I lift it to my nose.

It smells like her.

Drinking it down, I remember her and taste what freedom felt like if only for a moment. A sweet trickle followed by a cringing burn of regret. I drink the rest of the whiskey to drown that burning.

(NOW)

Bells snap the silence, ripping me away from Jay and dropping me back to now. The Bells! The final call for the festival! I run up the road seeing the boy emerge from the alley ahead of me. Reaching out, my fingers catch his shirt, but he slips through and runs faster away.

"Hide kid! You gotta hide!" Swiping at him again, I miss his shoulder. "Hide!" But he runs faster out of the orange haze of the streetlights into the bleak dusk and tall grass of the cliffs.

Ahead I see raging bonfire flames and smoke lacing the darkening sky. Shadows convulse and dance around the townsfolk watching the horizon at the cliff's edge. A pin prick of light pops in the sky as the first stars of night spring into sight.

We're here. The festival.

The boy stops. His ragged clothes rippling in the billowing gusts of salty sea air.

"You gotta-" grabbing his shoulder my hand passes through him. A cool mist wraps around me as the boy dissolves into vaper on the sea's breeze.

Blinking, the boy's gone, replaced a few feet away by Kyle. His face glistens in the fire light, slick and puffy from tears. A full beer falls from his hand, cracking on a rock as I remember standing here last night. Kyle and I watching the townsfolk setting up for the festival.

(THEN)

"Our last night here Theo!" Kyle clinks his beer to my bottle of whiskey.

"Cheers to that!" I laugh and suck down a swig.

"You all set to head out after the festival tomorrow?" Kyle points to the unlit bonfires rolling his eyes.

"Yeah, boat sold." I sigh "My life is in that suitcase. Pretty sad when you can get your whole life in one bag." I snicker but wonder…is that sad? Taking another gulp of whiskey to drown out the thought.

"Just think of it like, you ain't taking any baggage with you. Fresh start and all." Kyle points to his single bag. "Leaving all this bullshit and lies here. Shitty jobs, shitty parents, all that stays here." He takes a deep drag of his beer. "At least we can get drunk at the festival tomorrow while nothing happens and some poor bastard swings from the cliff." Kyle dances around, spilling his beer and howling spooky noises as laughter bubbles out of him.

"I don't know Kyle." I say. "You think it IS all bullshit?" I point out into the sea. "I mean, people have believed something's out there for a long time and…I don't know. Beliefs come from somewhere." Shrugging, sounding silly but questioning.

"Yeah, it came from somewhere. It came from the town elders wanting to stay the wealthy town elders. It came from people like my scum bag parents who don't believe any of this shit. They knew if everyone left, no one would pay their stupid tithe and they'd be broke or worse…" Kyle gasps and gets serious, "…have to get a job!"

We both bursts into laughs.

"Just drop your bag off in my car tonight so we can roll out right after sunset tomorrow." Kyle points to his red VW Beetle sitting on the street a few feet away.

I look to the stars wondering if wherever I end up, will the stars look the same? More stars appear as I realize I'm back at the festival, back from the memory.

(NOW)

Kyle runs to me, panic draining away his color. "What are you doing here!?" His voice strains to whisper.

"The rope broke." I pull on the frayed tatters still wrapped around my waist. "I've been trying to get up here but-"

"Why?" Kyle snags my arm. His face twists with the question, with the wonder why I didn't think that from the start.

Simple, emotionless words fall out of me.

"I'm the sacrifice for the festival. My life has led to this. If I'm not hanging over that cliff when the sun sets…" I look to horizon seeing the sun's last edges wriggling against the water. "…well, you know what they've told us."

"Everyone thinks you're down there." Kyle points to the cliff. "This festival is just some stupid shit to keep us all here. It don't matter if you're here. This…" he flaps around at the people watching the horizon, watching the ripples in the waves, chanting their songs, "is just some old story to keep people scared. They picked you because we were going to leave Theo. You know it. They wanted to hang you off that cliff for wanting more than this place. There's nothing out there! Nothing's going to destroy the town or the world or anything!"

Listening to the voices singing and chanting, I realize Kyle is the only person who gives a damn about me here. I've lived here my whole life, and no one thought twice about throwing me over that cliff, dangling like bait for whatever comes to feed at the festival. The village says the thing in the water brings us life and calm seas, but all I've ever been brought is doubt, being drunk and wandering through life. I've been stuck here sprinting towards death.

Picking up the rope, thinking about the boy, the boat, the bar, the car and knowing today has been my last day…until now.

Kyle points to his red Beetle on the street, still packed and ready outside the festival firelight.

"You can stay and die, or we can go and live." He slaps my arm then walks to his car leaving me on the edge of the bonfire light. I look to the townsfolk, knowing tomorrow they'll go back to their lives in this town. Tomorrow…tomorrow is a place where I've pushed everything in my life, adventure, love, happiness always assuming I'll have another tomorrow.

If I stay, there's no tomorrow and all those things will be left undone.

Who can I be tomorrow?

Getting in Kyle's car I look back to the horizon seeing the sun's last light devoured by the sea. The car starts and the boy, the boy running through the town, watches me with his stormy sea eyes. A slight grin cracks over his face as we drive away.

Far from town, we can see the bonfires going out. The chanting songs fade away. Only the sound of crashing waves can be heard now and the screaming howl of an angry storm approaching. Driving into the night, the stars begin to vanish as we get closer to Dublin. I roll down my window, stick out my head and wonder what the stars will look like when I get wherever I am going.

Author's Note:

The Wisp

2014-2019

This story was inspired by the village of Howth in Dublin Bay. Many years ago, my wife (not at the time but eventually) and I traveled there. I fell in love with the place. Howth is a common inspiration for my stories especially ones about fantasy or encountering ancient forces.

During our trip to Howth, another story formed in my journal called "At the Grave of R.L. Barret". That story was inspired by a teddy bear tied to a gravestone. In The Wisp, our main character stops at a tavern that is on the way to the grave of R.L. Barret which is in the ancient Saint Mary's Church and Cemetery.

This story to me was about leaving where you've always been. That can be a major challenge for people as well as a significantly freeing experience. Theo wants to escape but he feels bound to this place. Everything he knows is this place. His identify is wrapped up in this place and that makes leaving extremely challenging.

A common question I'm asked about this story is: What happened next? Referring to: was there a monster and did the monster come out of the sea and destroy everything. I leave that to your imagination.

Originally, this story was called "100ft Rope". It was inspired by a writing prompt to make up a story's title and then write the story. I was in a store and saw the label 100' rope, and said, hey that makes sense. Combining "The Lottery" by Shirley Jackson, the cliffs of Howth and escaping your hometown prison turned into The Wisp.

In my experience, people don't leave toxic places willingly. I'm thankful that there has always been a Wisp to help me escape even if that help was seeing what I've done in life or guiding me to someone who cares.

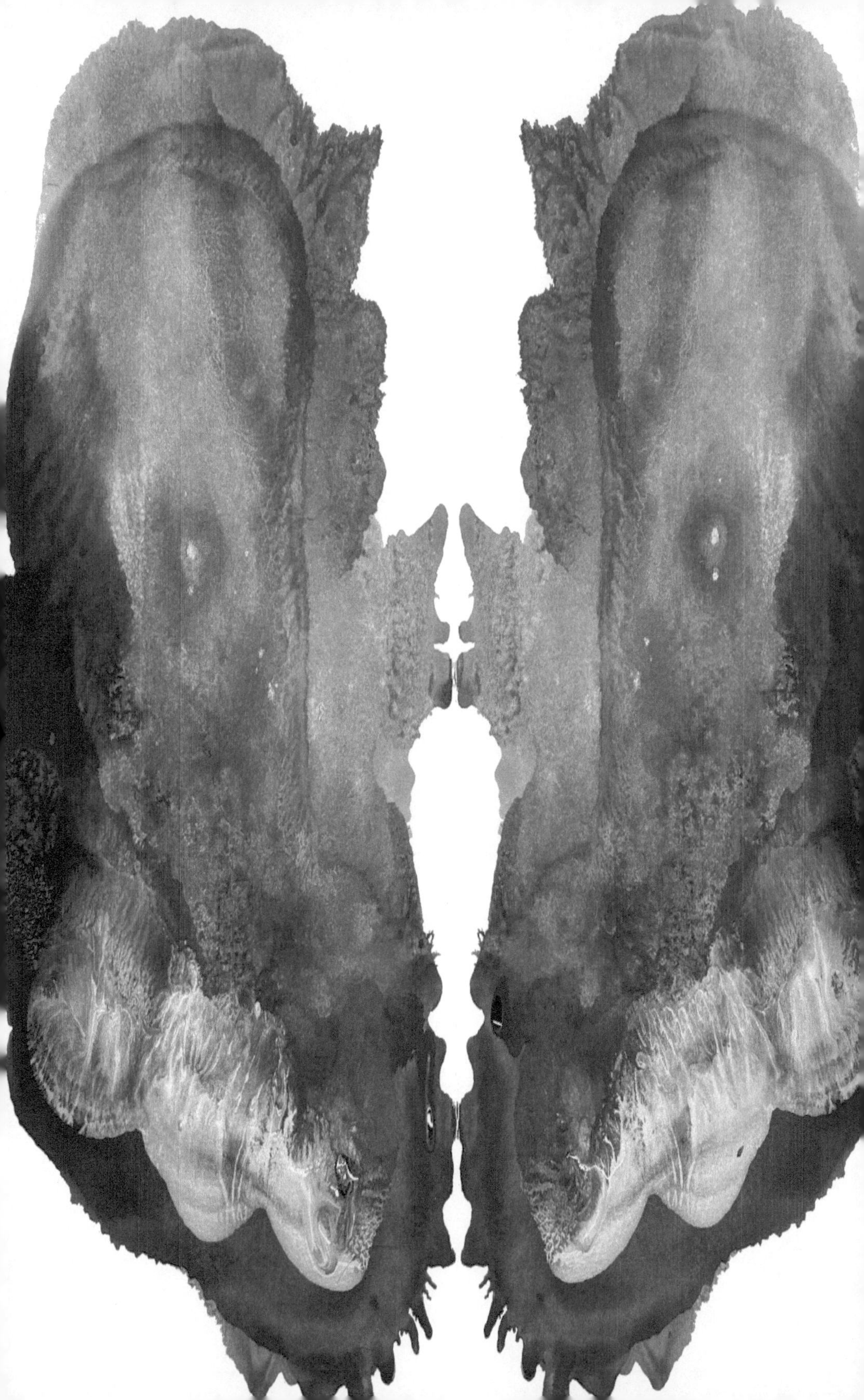

OLD JACK

Panic grips the fly
as the spider closes in.

Stuck in honey water,
the wings helplessly buzz
as the spider
springs in
for the kill.

The two wrestle,
but Old Jack
knows who will win.

He watches,
smirking,
leaning in to hear
the fly's pleading,
the spider's jaws crunching,
disappointed to hear nothing.

He sighs at the
fly's struggle,
the spider's inevitable victory.

Old Jack doesn't wait for the feeding to begin.
He flicks the spider through the tiny door
of his latest paper house.

Shutting the door
he locks it
with a piece of tape.

Smashing the fly,
Old Jack wipes off the honey water
and starts
a new house for
a new spider.

Humming to himself
Cruel Summer by Bananarama
he licks his fingers,
and plucks a page from the
pile of white paper.

Old Jack flattens it beside the dusty old book.
His nub of purple crayon
draws the symbols
from the dusty old book.

Loops and lines
and circles with stars
cover the paper.
Each stroke
leaving a waxy purple gash
on the face of the paper house.

"Old Jack."
he scoffs
interrupting the chorus
of Cruel Summer.

Muffled shouts come from the corner.
"Shut it!"
Old Jack says.

"Gotta concentrate."
His forehead creases
and cracks under the pressure
of the origami house construction.

He tapes the house together
to seal all the seams,
to keep what will be inside
from escaping.

Holding the house close to the old dusty book
he verifies his creation
against the illustration on the page.

He nods.
Satisfied.

Clacking wooden chair legs
rattle in the corner.

"Shut it!"
Old Jack barks.
But the corner doesn't shut it,
it muffles and mumbles
through the sock stuffed in the boy's mouth.
The boy in the corner
tied to the wooden chair.

Old Jack
puts the newly finished house down
and stomps over to the corner.
"What Donnie?"
Old Jack rips the sock
from the kid's mouth.

Donnie stretches his lips
finding his voice.
"Please Jacky, please let me go!"
Tears run down Donnie's face
into the sweat
or piss that soaks his clothes.

"Old Jack…"
The sock is punched into Donnie's mouth.
"likes to sit alone and read old books."
Old Jack smiles.
"What a loser…
Isn't that what you said?"

Donnie shouts through the sock
something sounding like "sorry"
something sounding like "please".
The clarity of this situation
hits Donnie in the face hard
as hard as the sock hit his teeth.

Screams for his mommy
break down to pleading sobs.

"Donnie don't be such a cry baby."
Old Jack says.

A grunt slips from him as he lifts
a paper house from his shelf.
The basement light glints off the
wax that now runs like tearful mascara.

This house was made days ago,
when Old Jack first learned how to make them.
The spider in this one
has been here for days
and has grown
heavy.

Old Jack wobbles carrying the house
as if it were the weight of a real house
containing real things,
heavy things,
inside.

"Baby Donnie."
Old Jack laughs.
"Baby Donnie likes to pick on Old Jack.
Baby Donnie thinks he's funny.
Baby Donnie likes to get the other kids
to make fun of Old Jack."

Old Jack puts the house down
in front of Donnie.

Sighs in relief.

"Baby Donnie made school horrible."

Old Jack replays the lunchroom incident
in his mind.
Remember and reaffirming
this is the right thing to do.

Whispers
slip towards Old Jack
from the work bench,
from the book.

Old Jack nods
his face
hardening.

"You said kids like me should be playing.
Only weirdos read.
You told the other kids to call me Old Jack
cause I'm like an old man.
Alone,
no friends,
a loser who reads all the time.
Well,
I read a book
that me showed me…"
He grins, snatches shining steel scissors
from his pocket
and waves them in Donnie's face.
"how to stop getting picked on by
people
like
you."
With each beat the scissors
bounce off Donnie's tear scarred cheeks.

Icy steel scissor blades
tangle in Donnie's eye lashes.
Old Jack pulls the blades but they're caught
in those long lashes the girls giggle over.

He pulls again,
Donnie's face jerks forward.
Old Jack twists
and rips the scissors back.

Donnie yelps
and yanks away.
Screaming,
pleading,
crying.

Old Jack clips the tape on the door
then taps twice.

KNOCK.

KNOCK.

Donnie looks at the house.
A paper house
marked with strange symbols
and bent in stranger angles
sitting a few feet away.

Old Jack knows something.
He knows something horrible
and Donnie can feel that secret
pulling on his eyes,
making them bulge as
the paper house's
door slowly open.

"Don't resist Donnie.
That just gets messy, and I already used up
all my parent's cleaning stuff."
Old Jack barks at Donnie,
frustrated that he'll have to use
allowance to buy new cleaning supplies.

Old Jack goes back to his workbench
and picks up another piece of paper
folding it with the concentration this work requires.

Soft peppy singing…
Wham's Wake Me Up Before You Go Go.
His shoulders shimmy as he sings
holding the crayon like a microphone.

Behind him
the chair clacks and taps
as Donnie shakes and
screams through the sock.

The wooden chair crashes on the concrete
Donnie's head hitting the floor
with the wet smashing of a dropped watermelon.

Muffled pleading
dissolves into shrieks
and gurgling
and choking.

Old Jack sighs
frustrated
singing louder.

Sudden quiet.

The same song
of the others
when they came over.

"You should have thought about this
before you picked on me Donnie."
Old Jacks drops the crayon nub on the worktable
and folds the newest house
to the tune of sloshing,
slurping and cracking bone.

He finishes the house
and turns around to see Donnie's
leg slurped like spaghetti
into the paper house on the floor.
Old Jack walks over to the house,
closes the door
and slides tape over the opening.

"Maybe they should have thought about that
before they called me Old Jack."
He smiles.

Grunting as he
lifts the house,
he places it beside the others
on the shelf.

"Jacky, dinner time!"
Mom calls from the stairs.
"Is Donnie joining us?"

"No Mom, he left already."
Old Jack answers with a chuckle.
"He said he was going home."

"Okay. Wash up
and get ready for tacos!"

"Sweet! Tacos!"
Old Jack jumps up.
Closes his book.

The old dusty book that
found him
when the kids
pushed him too far.

Walking by his shelf,
he pauses and looks at his collection.
Six houses
with spiders
or whatever they
became inside those houses.

Twenty more houses sit on his workbench.
"Yeah, my class should have thought about this
before they called me Old Jack."
He plucks the rusty chain for the light
returning the basement to empty blackness.

Only the dusty old book's faint purple dust,
the floating dust that comes from the pages,
can be seen shimmering in the darkness.

Old Jack rushes upstairs
ready to crunch into
Tuesday night
family dinner
tacos.

Pulling out his chair,
waving at a buzzing near his ear
Old Jack asks.
"Can Sarah come over tomorrow?"

                    "Will she stay for dinner?"

Old Jack smiles
as a fly lands on his taco.

"Probably not."

Author's Note:

Old Jack

2020-2021

This story started from a writing prompt about Paper Houses. Write a story about Paper Houses and what came to mind was that the Paper Houses were the house of a monster.

I liked the Lovecraftian idea of books being tomes of forbidden knowledge and thought about what would happen if a kid being bullied got his hands on such a book. When writing the story, I didn't know "Old Jack" was a kid. That part surprised me. I thought originally it was some creepy guy kidnapping kids but as the story unfolded and I discovered who Old Jack was, I was surprised.

You'll notice the purple crayon in this story. That is indeed a reference to Harold and the Purple Crayon. This is one of my favorite children's books and has been a prize in my house for years. While Harold uses his crayon for good, Jack in this story is not so kind or creative.

I read somewhere that a short story should be a great first chapter or last chapter in a longer story. Old Jack is probably going to grow into a larger story. This story seems to be the first chapter of something much larger. I love the characters and have a feeling that this story takes place during the Satanic Panic of the 1980s. That will be a fun setting between everything being evil, stranger danger, and the general "me" focus of the 1980s, this story could really grow legs…or whatever might grow in the Paper Houses.

The next story, Signature, has some strong ties to Old Jack. I leave it to you to understand which story comes first and whether or not they are related.

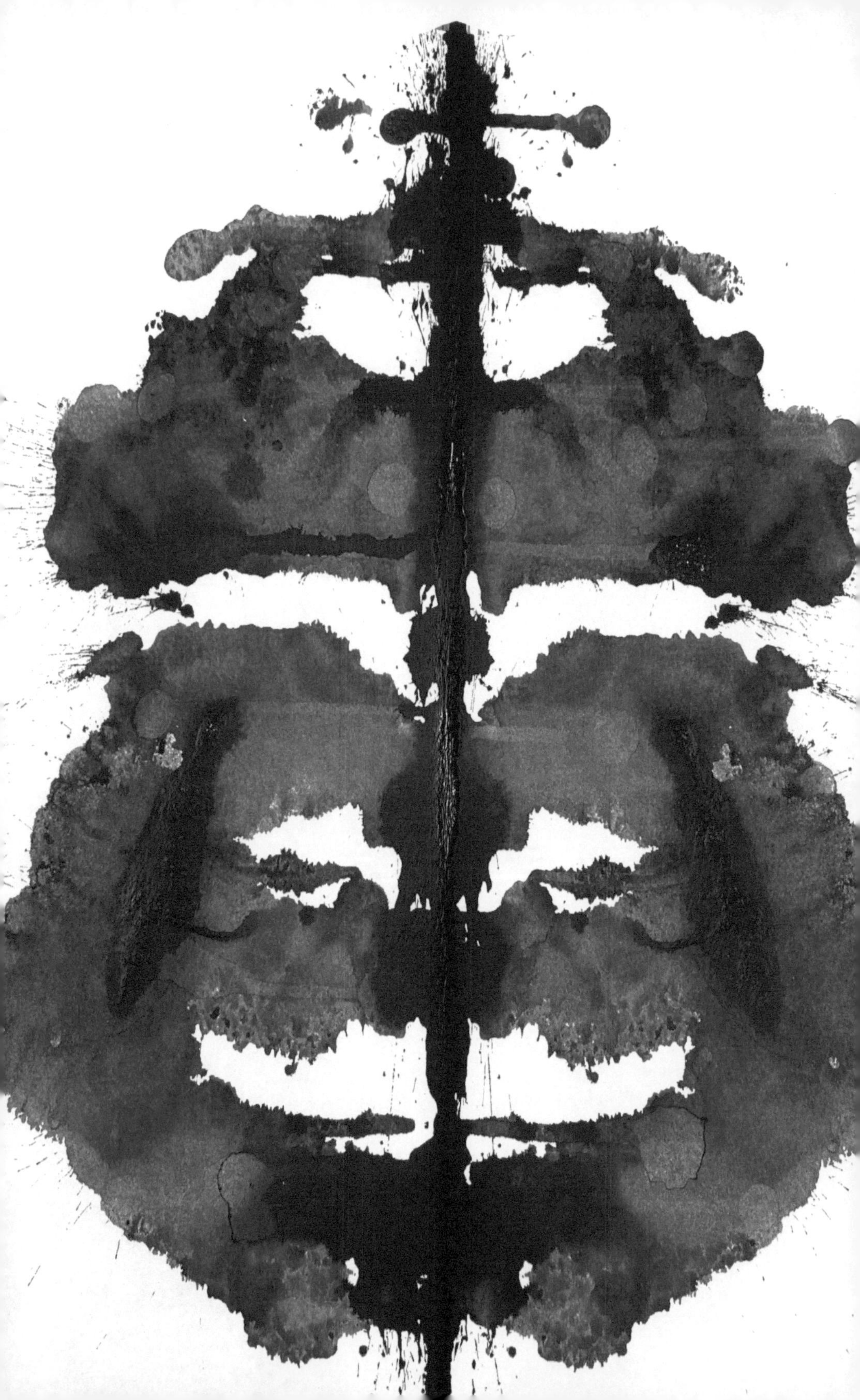

SIGNATURE

Left Behind

"Where's my backpack mom?"
I search my room.

Sweeping up each sweater
and shirt on my floor
I throw it all in my closet.

I don't remember when my room
was this clean.
But still no backpack.

No book.

"It's wherever you left it."
Mom shouts back.

"Unhelpful…"

Where did I leave it?

Replaying yesterday afternoon
I got off the bus,
got a snack…

The kitchen!

On my desk,
faint dust outlines
where the book has been each night.

I didn't realize
my room was so dusty.

I swipe a streak in it
and flick some of the dust off.
Wiping the rest
on my shirt.

Downstairs in the kitchen,
I retrace my steps.
Coming in the side door,
stopping at the counter,
getting a bowl of cereal.

No backpack
around the counter.

I slept on the couch
after that.

No backpack
around the couch.

I don't remember
anything after the couch.

"Mom, I can't find my backpack!"

"Did you bring it home?"
She rounds the corner
hosing her hair down
with hairspray.

The cloud clears around her
as the memories flood back to me.

I didn't bring it home.

I LEFT IT AT SCHOOL…

"What's wrong sweetie?"
Mom says.
"You look like
a goose walked over your grave."
She chuckles
and goes to the fridge.

Breathe.

Breathe.

How could I be so stupid?
I…phew…I

I had my backpack at dismissal,
I visited Amy in her English class,
I put my backpack down at my normal English desk.

Then I wasn't feeling well.
I got sick again
and ran to the bathroom.

Then…Mrs. Greene took me to the bus
from the bathroom.

Going to the kitchen
my hands flapping the sweat off.
"Mom, did you see my backpack last night?"

Standing in the fridge door
she shakes her head
while swigging from the milk carton.

"Which tie honey?"
Dad asks.

Mom ducks her face
into her pink sleave
and wipes away the milk mustache
before dad catches her
committing the crime she always
yells at him about.

The fridge closes
as mom helps dad with his tie.

I shiver
thinking about
someone finding my backpack,
finding the book.

What if someone took it?

What if…

what it someone

read it?

They'd think I'm one of those
Satanists that was on the news
last week.

Mom and dad will freak out.

They'll put me in
an institution
like that kid who disappeared.

The kid who dropped the book.

"Don't miss the bus kiddo!"
Mom says as her and dad
walk out to the car.

"Wait!
Can I get a ride to school
early?"

Mom sways backwards
balancing in those
too high heels.

"Yeah, let's go."
She motions me out.

I run to her.
My fingers twist, slip and roll
as nervous sweat slicks
my palms.

How could I forget?

My stomach rolls with my fingers
loosening my knees
and I stumble.

Mom catches me.

"I'll…"
Vomit catches in my throat.
"be right there. Just gotta…"
My chest heaves.
"bathroom."

Running
closing the door
dropping to the toilet
letting my stomach pump out
the puke that keeps coming.

"You okay sweetie?"
Mom calls from outside the door.

"Yeah, mom."
I choke down the sick.
"Just choked on something."
Spitting
gray sludge
into the toilet.

Same as it has been.

Washing my face,
I flush
and rush out.

Mom's worried
but I smile.

"Just, nervous."

I've been
nervous
a lot lately.

Nervous
since
I found the book.

The Ride

Watching the street go by
I think about

who
might have seen the book.

Who
would go into my bookbag?

No one.

"You know sweetie,"
Mom starts in her
afterschool special voice.
"you are beautiful how you are."

She nods
swats dad
he nods agreement.

"You don't need to change
anything about you."

Mom smiles and reaches
back to rub my shoulder.
The new car is too big
and she can't quite reach.

"I know mom."
I nod
and look back out
the window.

"You don't need to lose weight
or anything. You are perfect
how you are."
She affirms.

I nod.

"What are you talking about?"
No one would bother
the book.

No one would dig through
my backpack.

Everything's fine.

"Some people,"
Mom shifts in her seat
looking straight ahead.
"try to loose weight by
making themselves sick.
But you don't do that
do you?"

She wiggles to push out the words.
"You are perfect and don't need
to loose weight."

"Uh, okay. Yeah. Thanks."

"You okay Jenny?"
Dad asks
breaking mom's confused attempt
at an intervention.

"Yeah, everything's fine."
I nod.
"Just, nervous."

"Well, keep those
butterflies in your belly."
Dad chuckles to himself
rubbing the leather steering wheel.
"Don't throw up in my new ride."

Mom whacks him
knocking his hand from the wheel
as he yelps.

The new car smell is
choking.
He keeps saying
this is the first new car
he's ever been able to buy.

It is a nice car.
He got it after the promotion,
after I found the book.

My stomach gurgles.
NO

I swallow hard
stomping the butterflies
into smearing pulp.

"I'm just saying Jenny,
you don't need to make yourself
sick."
Mom picks back up.

I'm not making myself sick.
The book said this could happen,
that the energy of the book
could create

discomfort

while my body adapts
to the energy.

But its an old book.

Not magical.

Just a weird old book.

There's no energy.
I'm just sick.

The boys are looking at
Playboys,
I'm looking at
mystical symbols and
ancient words.

At least the pictures in my book
aren't porn.
Just symbols.
Anatomical diagrams.

"No, I'm not doing that mom."
I keep my eyes out the window
seeing a flicker of purple
in the reflection.

Looking again,
nothing's there.
Probably just flowers
in some garden.

"Everything's fine mom."
The words
fade between us.

I should have left the book at home
but I just can't stop reading it.
I can't let it go.

How could that boy leave it?

My hands jitter
as my fingers remember the leather cover,
the brittle pages crinkling,
smelling the musty scent of aged paper.

"Something funny?"
Mom asks,
her voice cheering.

In the window
I see I'm smiling
"No, just a good memory."

Everything's fine.

Everything will be fine.

Decisions

Dad pulls around
the parking lot
dropping me off.

"Remember sweetie,
you're perfect how you are."
Mom whispers back to me.

I smile
nod
"Everything's fine."

People cluster
in the school
courtyard.

I meld with them
until I see
Amy and Audrey
by the flag pole.

Amy is pulling on her jacket,
again.

Her eyes are red,
her cheeks slick.

Joining them,
"What's wrong?"

"Ruzzo's an asshole."
Audrey nods toward
Joey Ruzzo's
flock of deviants.

Joey
bobbles around
like a bloated
cow.

His friends
follow his lead
like fat zombies
mimicking their master.

They make
sloppy sloshing
eating noises
and point
at Amy.

"Assholes."
I gently hold Amy's arm
and walk her to the crowd
by the doors.

We melt
into the mass of bodies
sleepily waiting to
start school.

"He's an asshole.
Forget him."

Amy sniffs back a tear
lifting her face
letting her tears fall back
into her eyes.
"I can't do anything about it."
Amy tugs on her jacket
straining the canvas.
"My dad says its genetic."

"Amy just ignore those idiots."
Audrey says
turning her attention to her nails.
Her manicure more interesting than
Amy's pain.
"Just remember, they'll drop out
and be losers all their life."
Audrey takes out her compact
and checks her lips.
"This is the best life they'll
ever have and you'll be fabulous
with a college education."

Amy smiles at that.
A reminder of her future
is just what she needed.

Joey Ruzzo keeps at it.

I don't understand.

He was a sweet kid.
Amy and him use to swing together
and play.
He beat up that kid who made fun of her
in third grade.

He came to my birthday party
a few years ago.
Gave me the Barbie
I wanted.

His mom said
he picked it for me.

He was nice.
I guess
people
change.

When did he change?
Was it last year?
Two years ago?
How fast can someone change?

Is it one
big decision
to change or an
accumulation
of small things?

BONG!
BONG!
BONG!

The doors open
and we flood in.

Interception

Bodies crush against me
as everyone pushes to where
they want to be.

Some are going to homeroom.

Some to a boyfriend's locker.

Some to breakfast.

For me,
only the English room exists.

I squeeze and push and shove
to break through.

"Ms. Fields,"
I turn,
Mr. Coldstone
comes up behind me.
"can we talk?"

He found it.

He found it
and now he wants to

talk.

"Uh…yeah…sure."
He motions towards a classroom,
my home room.
I plop down
steeling myself.

He leans over.
"I need to talk to you
about something serious."
He takes out a notebook
and pen.

Scripted responses quickly
appear in my mind.

I didn't know what it was.

I didn't look at it.

I didn't do anything.

Some kid dropped it.

Sucking in my breath
readying the barrage of
explanations
denials…

"Have you
thought about summer jobs?"
He asks.

"I didn't do…"
Wait.
"What?"

He leans away from me.
"Summer jobs?
Summer is coming up
and I wanted to recommend you
for a job at the bookshop
in town."
He writes something down.

"My friend is the owner
and I know you love books
so I thought this could be great."

"Oh…"
Blowing out,
sinking into my chair,
chuckling awkwardly,
"Oh, yeah. That would be great.
I don't have anything lined up
and was just going to spend
the summer
reading."

Popping up straight
hearing what I said,
"I mean reading for school.
Not reading anything
that isn't school related
or anything."

Mr. Coldstone nods.
Keeping his distance
he hands me the note,
and walks away.

I follow him to the door
stopped again
by Mrs. Greene,
my homeroom teacher.

"Ms. Fields!"
She grins.
Her braces are prison bars
that slam shut over the exit.
"Great to see you
here so early.

You must be here to catch up
on all your late work."

Ugh…
That's right.

The homework from last week.

I don't have time
for homework.
Not now,
Not at night.
That is time for the book.

"I, uh, left my backpack
in another class."
I point around her
but those braces,
that grin
block the exit.
"Can I just go get it?"

"No need. I have paper
and the assignment right here."
Like magic, Mrs. Greene plucks
the assignment from her folder.

Was she waiting for this?
Her smile says
yes.

"Pencils too."

Two pencils appear
from the magical folder.

I nod,
politely take my seat
and start the assignment.

US. Government.

Ugh…

Tick, tick, tick,
question one,
tick, tick, tick,
question two,
tick, tick, tick,
the clock devours time
as the questions drag on.

The worksheets take forever
and Mrs. Greene taps her pencil,
clicking wood on wood
faster and faster
keeping pace with the seconds
that are keeping me here
away from my…the book.

"Where was the battle of…"
Errrr!
The tapping,
the ticking,
I scribble answers
half thoughts,
good enough answers.

I need the book,
not an A.

Crinkling the papers
I run them to Mrs. Greene
and toss them on her desk.

Turning to the door,
traffic in the hall is thin.

"Ms. Fields."
Mrs. Greene points up
to the ceiling.

I look up
seeing nothing
then,

BONG!
BONG!
BONG!

Homeroom
has started.

"Everyone in your seats please."
Mrs. Greene says
with a smile.

Her gaze settles on my
worried eyes,
twisting hands,
dripping palms.

"Ms. Fields, get your assignments
done on time and you get free time.
No assignment, no free time…"
Her braces glint in the
green school lights.
"Your decisions matter dear."

She shrugs
as I shamble back
to my seat.

Sealed

I get to English class,
finally,
and there it is.

Wiping my palms dry,
pushing through the people
leaving first period English,
I get to my desk.

To my backpack.

It's open.

I suck in a clattering breath,
it catches in my chest
shaking my guts.

Dropping my hand into the bag
my fingers graze over the
slick black leather cover.

It's there.

Shewwww!
I blow out
the morning's
tension.

Shoulders drop.

Worry dissolved.

My fingers trace
the symbol on the leather cover
feeling the lines and forms.

Tingling slides up my fingers
and over my spine
as a moan slips out.

Yes, it feels that good
to have the book back.

Pulling out the black leather book,
I need to see it.
I open it
the first page,
The Page of Names,

and there it is.

Gouging the page in a canyon
of pink pen ink:

JOEY RUZZO WAS HERE

The words

twist

my

insides.

Each letter
cranking the coil
of my nerves
liquifying my knees.

Tunnel vision
sucks me into
the signature.

Feeling the wrinkled page
the gored pen stroke
scrawled in eye searing pink
defying the nature of this book.

All the world
is devoured by the void
surrounding this absolute statement

JOEY RUZZO WAS HERE

Squawking laughter from the doorway
cracks my daze
as Joey Ruzzo
points at me
laughs at me

his friends laugh at me

his friends point

I rub the pink ink
trying to push it out the paper
trying to erase it
but I can't.

White finger tips
push into the crinkling paper
crackling like electricity
like potential energy building
ready to explode.

He laughs harder
at my struggle
to save his life.

"You idiot!"
I scream.

He laughs
rocking back
caught by his friend.
Blood fills Joey's face
as he grabs his stomach.

"You idiot!"
I rush him
smacking his face
he keeps laughing
ducking and running away.

"You asshole!"
I shout
grabbing my stomach.

"Ms. Fields!"
Mr. Coldstone barks.
"We don't use that language here
no matter how true it might be."

The class laughs.

I drop to my knees
white puke exploding out of me.

People gasp
and shout.

Someone else pukes.

                    "Ms. Fields!"
                    Mr. Coldstone runs to me,
                    holding the other students back away.

                    "Billie, go to the office!
                    Get the nurse!"

Everyone panics.

Another bucket of barf crashes out of me
pooling on the floor
between my hands.

The dust from this morning
is still on my fingers.

Someone else pukes.

The smell seizes my stomach
dumping an erruption of pale oatmeal
between my fingers.

It coats my hands
and knees
and spreads
no, not spreads,
crawls.

It's not pooling
its crawling away

Falling
to the side
all goes dark.

Thank God!

I didn't land
in a splash.

Everything's Fine

"Where's my backpack?"

The nurse pushes me
back to the bed.

"Where is it?"
My eyes sprint around the room
looking for the pink Jansport
holding the black leather book.

"Calm yourself deary."
Nurse Hannah wheezes.
She holds my arms down
straining for control.
"Just calm down,
you're in my office."

There it is.
My backpack.
The book, winking to me
in a crack of the zipper.

"Can I have my backpack?"

Nurse Hannah springs back from me
letting my arms free.
I slide around her and grab
my backpack.
Slipping my fingers into the zipper hole
I sigh taking in the comforting air
of knowing the book is back to me.

Mom walks in.

Nurse Hannah is still recoiled
from me on the bed.
Mom looks to her,
then to me
curled around my backpack,
puke-soaked knees,
crusty clumpy hair
where I didn't make it
past my own pool of sick
when I passed out.

I squeeze my bag
still feeling
the book.

Mom and Nurse Hannah
go into another room
and talk.

Words like
"Jenny is a good girl."
and
"she isn't sick"
leak through the cracked door.

They talk
while I read
taking the moment
to reconnect with what I missed
last night.

Mom comes out
and takes me to our old car.
We drive home.

"What's going on Jenny?"
Mom reaches for my knee
pulling away before touching
the wet spot.

"Nothing."
I turn to the window.

"Well, nothing's been happening
for a few days now."
She says.

"Everything's fine."
I mumble.

"Throwing up twice in one day
is fine? Not sleeping is fine?
Passing out on the couch
because you're so tired you
can't get up is fine?"
We're speeding up.
Mom's old car engine grunts
and gargles to keep accelerating.

"Just, a lot going on."

"Is it your friends?"
Mom pleads.
"Are they telling you to do something
you don't want to do?"

I watch the yards go by.
All of them the same
as are the houses
and cars
and people.

Everyone here
looks the same.

Acts the same.

Why did the book
pick me?

Did I find it
or did it find me?

Did it hear me
say I wanted something
more?

"Everything's fine mom."
I look to her
seeing her age,
tears creasing through
crows feet.

"Drugs?"
She shakes her head.
"Are you on drugs?"
She pats the steering wheel
with her palm,
quickly,
pat, pat, pat.
"You know to 'Just Say No', right?"

"We raised you better than drugs."

Not a question.
Statement.

"I'm not on drugs.
Just got a lot on my mind."
Like Joey Ruzzo
signing his life away.

Like a book
that grants wishes.

Like finding out
magic is real
and it's making me sick
and I'm puking living liquid.

"Just don't worry mom.
I'm fine."
I tuck back into the window.

        "I'm your mother.

        I worry."
        She says.

"I said I'm fine.
You need to listen to me!

I'm fine.

Everything's fine!"

The car is quiet.

In the window
mom's reflection
shows a hanging mouth
and free flowing tears.

She clears her throat
and nods.

"You're grounded."
She says.
Calm.

"Fine."
I smile
thinking of being locked
in my room
with
the book.

I have a lot of reading to do.

Joey added his name
to the Page of Names.
There's got to be a way
to save him.

This can be undone.

I just need to read more.

Dig deeper.

He's an asshole now,
but there's a good person in him.
I know it.

This was a stupid prank
and that shouldn't be with him
forever.

Just a prank,
a bad decision,
but the Page of Names…

The Collector.

Joey signed his life away
but I can help him.
The book can save him.

He'll be fine.

Everything's fine.

Research

Mom escorts me
to my room.

"Jenny,"
she sighs,
"we're here for you.
We love you."

Why did she say that?

There's nothing
wrong.

Nothing's changed.

"I know mom."
I nod.
"I'm sorry I yelled."

She sniffles,
nods and waves me in
for a hug.

I go to her
and she squeezes me
popping my back
in a tremor
rumbling up my spine.

Mom jumps back
loosening
and looking into my eyes
for
pain.

It didn't hurt.

The popping eruption
was more like
a realignment.

The squeezing
adjusted me
to let out
the tension of the day.

"I'm okay.
Honestly."

Mom looks to my hands
where the book flips
between eager palms
ready to read.

Ready for her to leave.

When did I take that out
of my backpack?

I hold it
as still as I can
"Oh, just homework.
Reading."

Flashing the book.

"I'll leave you to it.
I'm here when you want to talk."
Mom goes to the door
and waits.

The dust frame on my desk
calls for the book
to be opened
to be read.

Placing it in the frame,
opening it to the first page
I sit
and feel
the pink gouge again.

Each page crackles
under my fingers.
When will a page just crumble?
They're only held together
with this purple dust and dirt.

How could Joey look at this book,
the slick black leather,
the blotchy midnight ink
writing and drawings,
the pictures of corpses
and constellations
and say…Yep, I'm going to mess with this.

Leaning back,
I wonder
why I messed with this book?

"I love you Jenny."
Mom's voice
startles me.

She's still at the door.

And still is,
waiting.

"Oh, yeah, I love you too."
I smile and watch for her to leave.

Another moment lingering,
her shoulders slump
and she leaves me
to the book.

Whispers
pull me back
to my desk.

Looking around,
seeing no one,
probably just mom's voice
echoing in the house.

In the book,
I flip to the section
about the Page of Names.

My finger drifts
over the passage.

Adding someone to the Page of Names will add them to The Collector's list. You must add the name, mean to add it and envision the victim clearly while writing. Any ambiguity in your thoughts, any doubt during the signature process will result in The Collector coming to you for clarity. Obtaining clarity occurs through a psionic link to The Collector who will scour your thoughts for the person and anything else it can add to its collection. This is undesirable for most people.

To avoid this, have the person you wish to add write their own name. Signing one's own name is a commitment with the intent and clarity The Collector requires. To get someone to sign their name…

"Damn it."
I whisper to the book.

Who is The Collector?

I skim through pages
stopping on the drawing
of eyes under an old bed.

The page's title:
THE COLLECTOR

The Collector is a shadow fey who is obsessed with gathering spiritual energy. It collects the souls of those in the Page of Names. The Collector comes to the Named while sleeping through doorways under where the Named sleeps. This has led to the monster under the bed fear. The Controller can summon The Collector to bargain for the soul…

Blah blah blah.

Scanning
the ancient pages
carefully lifting each page
sliding it over the next.

Ah, here…

That's it. I'll just explain
what happened
to The Collector.

No need to bargain or anything,
just explain.

It was an accident.

He didn't do it on purpose
and I didn't want him to do it
it just kind of happened.

Reading on
I glance to the darkness
pooling under my bed.

The arm of a gray sweater
reaches out from that darkness.
One arm claws towards me
the other held back under the bed.

Is it escaping
or trying to reach me?

"It's just a sweater.
And you're just a slob."
I shake away the thought
standing to pull it out
and throw it on the laundry pile.

Reaching for the sweater
I stop
when it wiggles.

Did it wiggle?

Stepping back to the book,
to my desk.

Watching the sweater,
one arm reaching out
twisted and bent
in car accident angles.

Did it wiggle?

Did it reach for me?

The pile of laundry in my closet
has tumbled over from this morning.
Did I miss this sweater?

Inching towards my bed
climbing over my footboard
I look to the sweater arm
waiting for another wiggle,
any movement.

Whispering
snaps my eyes
back to the book.

What did it say?

Nothing,
it didn't say anything.
Just heard mom talking
downstairs.

"This is stupid."
I swipe down
to scoop up the sweater
and rip it up from under my bed.

It wraps around my arm
but that's
normal.

Clothes do that.
They wrap around you
when you snatch them up.

I tug it away from my arm
and throw it into the closet.
The sweater slinks down the pile
slipping all the way to the floor
where the arms reach for me.

"Jenny! Dinner!"
Mom calls from downstairs.

I fall off my bed.

Cringing from the sweater, from the arms
reaching for me to snap me up
devour me

but the sweater doesn't pounce on me,
it doesn't jump up and rush to claw me
it just lays on the floor.

Because it's a sweater.

I shake out the stupid thoughts.

Laying on the floor,
noticing the sun's gone down
my room is dark.

On my ceiling is a universe
of purple dust
looking like stars.

The dust
floats up from my desk
from the book.

Waving my hand over it
the dust clings to me
like pollen on a car.

I flick it off,
but it stays.

Stuck to me.

       "Jenny! Come on down!"

"Coming!"

I close my door
and try to wipe off
the dust.

In Me

The swishing and squeaking
of toothbrush on teeth
is hypnotic.

I stare in the mirror
listening to the rhythm
of my nightly teeth cleaning
ritual.

In the mirror
I see the shapes
and sketches
of the book.

Summoning spells for monsters,
gateways for demons,
prisons for angels,
graves for ghosts.

So many stories.

Many of people
making deals.

The deal always goes bad.
Things always end badly
in those stories.

Cautionary tales?

In the mirror
I look for the purple dust
from the book.

No sign on my skin,
just me getting paler.

I need more sun.

No sign in my hair,
just my hair getting thinner.

I need some new conditioner.

Pushing my face closer to the mirror
I fog it over
examining my mouth,
my ears,
my nose.

"Good night kiddo."
Dad gives me a hug.
"Ow!"
he springs back.
Carefully approaching for another hug.
"Your bones stabbed me."
He squeezes.
No popping from me this time.

"Straight to bed."
He points to my eyes.
"Looking worn out."

I nod
and smile
like I'm supposed to.

Gargling through
toothpaste I spit and say
"Love you Dad."
like I'm supposed to.

Back to the mirror,
seeing the bags under my eyes
but nothing new.
Long nights of study
built those, the book
just added a bit more-

Leaning closer to the mirror
a fleck of purple
catches the bathroom lights.

A fleck of purple
in my brown eyes.

Not kind of purple,
not purplish
but glowing dust from the book purple.

Another fleck floats into my view.

And another.

Pulling my eye wide
pressing myself into the mirror
fogging over the glass with my breath.
Swiping away the moisture.

More flecks of dust are
in my eye.

The flecks aren't floating
they are crawling.
Scuttling on little legs.
Clamping little pinchers into my iris,
burrowing in and out
of the brown.

Erupting from the mud coloring
creeping to another area
and boring into my eye
again.

My toothbrush falls.

                          "Watch out Jenny!"
                          Mom cries.

I spring back
foaming at the mouth
screaming
spraying mom with toothpaste.

She recoils
from the white strands thrown
across her night shirt.

The teddy bear on her blue shirt
now foams at the mouth,
dribbling white puke

like me
at school.

"Nothing!"
I shout
preempting any questions.

Looking at nothing.

Seeing nothing.

Doing nothing.

"What? You just sprayed toothpaste
on my new pajamas!"
She brushes off the slimy goo.

"Just got startled."
I pick up the toothbrush
and spit into the sink.

A blob of white
crashes into the basin.
Red strings lace through
the blob.

Smiling in the mirror
I see pooling blood
around my teeth
clinging to my gums
trying to crawl back in.

Like the flecks
in my eyes.

"Brush softer sweetie."
Mom points to the spit.
"And take care of yourself."

She flashes me a knowing nod
and sad eyes.

"I'll call Doctor Miller
for a checkup in the morning."
Mom pats my arm.

I should smile
so I do.

When did the flecks start?

The moisture smears across the mirror
as I wipe the fog away for a clearer look.

The purple things skitter around my eyes
with intent
with focus
burrowing
vanishing.

Thin hair.

Pale skin.

Pointy bones.

Puking.

Now,
purple things in my eyes,
bleeding gums.

When did this start?

But,
I know when.

When it found me.

Negotiations

Lights go out
in the house.

Only the hallway light
remains.

Mom keeps that on
"for emergencies".
Dad and I laugh,
like we won't find a light switch
in an emergency,
but tonight I'm thankful.

The hallway
casts a slice of light
across my floor
dividing my bedroom
in two spaces.

The space where
my stuffed animals are,
where my laundry is piled.

And the space where
the book and my bed
sit waiting for tonight's
parlay.

Could I just get up
and leave?

Leave Joey Ruzzo to his fate?

Leave the book here
and sleep downstairs
and forget all this
craziness.

Listening careful,
hearing no more footsteps
or bathroom visits
or checking the doors,
I roll and peek over
the edge of my bed.

Darkness.

The sweater is gone,
it is on the other side of my room
the side with the stuffies and clothes.

Looking to the sweater,
it cringes away from the hall light
bunched and balled in the corner.

I stand
letting my feet sink
into the soft,
warm carpet.

The door is a step away,
the light is a step away.

The book
sits closed on my desk,
dust floating up
wandering onto the footboard
of my bed.

Reaching for my door,
finding the handle

I turn the handle
and silently close the door
driving away
the hallway light.

I lie down
looking to the purple dust stars
gathering on my ceiling.

Have I been breathing that?

It was on my footboard,
probably in my bed.

I've been sleeping in it,
touching it,
breathing it…?

Was there something in the book
about this dust?
I haven't seen anything.

The carpet welcomes me
wrapping around me
as I scootch towards my bed.

Lining my body up,
my stomach presses against
the bed frame.

Tight squeeze.

Breathing deep.

I wiggle under the metal frame
feeling the claw of a steel spring
grabbing my shoulder.

It's cold as it hits my skin
but burns as I push past it.
My shirt rips
and sticks to where the spring
broke the skin.

Pushing deeper into the bed,
the mattress
presses down on my chest
bulging through taunt wire framing.

I turn my head towards the darkness
so my face will fit
as I slide further.

Every breath is constricted
by the bed frame squishing me.

Soft carpet compacts
to a matted tangle below me.
It doesn't comfort against
the hard floor
but instead, becomes a bed of fingers
twisting and writhing to hold me up.

I think of The Collector,
like the book said.

I say the words,
like the book said.

"Collector, Collector,
speak to me of your collection."

Breathing slow.

Only shallow breaths allowed by the
mattress pushing down on me
like someone is lying
on my bed.

I long blink to see something,
anything,
other than the blackness
under my bed.

"Collector, Collector,
speak to me of your collection."

Drawing a deep breath
the air warmer now
freezing as it hits my throat.

My stomach can't take in the air.
The bed frame slowly sinks into me
the fingers under me pushing back.

I can't breathe...

Gasping,

"Collector, Collector,
speak to me of your collection."
Straining the last words out.

Pressing my eyes closed
the dark vanishes as a light show
ripples in my mind.

I read about this in science class.

Phosphines in my eyes,
electrical charges in my retinas,
a totally natural occurrence
not magical sparks,
not the world exploding out of existence
not a portal to another world.

Just electrical charges.

Trying to breathe
dragging in steaming humid air
thick
suffocating.

The air grows hotter
on my face
the carpet is warm,
burning.

Sucking in the damp hot air
I can breathe again.

Opening my eyes,
the mattress is above me
further away
as I fall
falling away from the taunt wire frame
falling with the floor,
the carpet of fingers fitting the curves of my back.

 Needling legs tap over my stomach.

I look down
but can't move my head.
My eyes drop to see
shadowy wisps
reaching over me,
finger nails are the needles.
They squeeze around me.

The floor ripples,
no, it breathes
drawing a deep breath
rattling as if choking
through a torn wet rag.

"You seek my collection?"
Hot wet words splash
over my cheek.

The Collector
is behind my head,
wrapped over my shoulder
breathing, wheezing
in my ear.

A pale light
descends above me
with a faint glow,

a calming glow,
in my view.

I breathe
feeling The Collector
tightening around me
as I inhale
and loosening
as I exhale.

The light
pulses with my breath
and The Collector's tension.

Joey Ruzzo,
the good kid,
the kid who came to my party
climbs into my mind
and reminds me why I'm here.

"No. There was a mistake.

Someone added their name
to your list."
Trying to find calm for my voice
but all the calm
has evacuated my heart
like cats escaping a burning building.

"Joey Ruzzo didn't know what he was doing.
He made a mistake."

The floor under me,
The Collector's body
bounces in ragged laughter.

Its body moves in disjointed
sections like the lobsters
in the super market tank.

"What is done,
is done."
The Collector whispers.
"He chose his part.
As you did yours."

Stiffening at that
stretching to look it in the eyes.
"No, I didn't want him to
write his name
in the book."

My arms strain against
The Collector's grip
and the light above me
grows brighter
grows

calmer.

I sigh
as it pulses.

Breathing

Slow.

"He thought he was ruining the book."
The words drip dreamily from me
and I hear them as if
someone else said them.
"He thought he was pranking me.
I left the book but didn't mean-"

                                        "Didn't mean to use it?"
                                        The Collector titters.
                                        "Didn't mean to use the book?"
                                        The light above me fades
                                        to black.

Thumping heart beats
play drums in my ears
as I wonder what it knows.

My face is hot
but not from the sweaty breath
of The Collector.

It knows.

It knows
I asked the book
for my dad's promotion.

I was just playing around,
just exploring,
trying it out.

I didn't think
it would work.

"I didn't-"

                                        "Didn't mean to get the benefits
                                        from the book?"
                                        The Collector titters again
                                        its body wriggling in segments
                                        under me.

It laughs like a stranger
in an afterschool special.

Laughs like they're about to
do something
to the girls they lure
into their vans

or basement

or…

bedroom.

"No, I did."
My body relaxes
letting go
knowing it knows
what I did.

There is no point
in arguing.

I helped my dad.
Yes, I did it.

"He signed his name."
The Collector states
matter of fact.
"You used the book
and awoke its power."
It says flowing logic
to the inevitable conclusion.
"He should not have signed the book."

"Is there anything
that can save him?"
I whisper
softly
fearing the answer.

Is it true…
what is done, is done?

                              "Yes. There is always another way."
                              The Collector says.

Its needling fingers
loosen and caress the gash
torn open by the rusty spring.

A stuttered breath
leaks out of The Collector in
swampy
hot
air.

Kai Felton
quaked like that
when he kissed me
at homecoming.

When his hands
slipped under my sweater.

Clenching my body
the needle fingers snap down
digging into me
as the light pulses on over me.

The soft glow
drags my mind away from the hot breathes,
from the needles slowly digging in
to find a vein…

Whispering fills my ear
drowning my racing heart
with

thoughts

and words.

Those words pry into my mouth
and dance through my lips
seizing all the muscles in my body
to contract
and then

Explode.

A wave of purple
erupts from inside me
plucking the needles from my skin,
shutting off the light,
The Collector drops me
and I float back up to the bed frame.

Warbling screeches
replace the heart beat in my ears
as The Collector
recoils from me.

Frustrated sighs
burn my neck
as the needles
find a looser grip on me.

The book?

"Let us keep this between us."
The Collector says
cautiously,
painfully.
"You need not get it involved again."

"I'll decide that."
The words come through me.
I am the vessel
of strength.

The book?

I throb with
a cold energy
seeing the purple dust
drift up from my body.

"Let us start again."
The Collector's voice
turns to legal speak.
"The named, that is Joey Ruzzo,
may be released from their obligation
if the Controller, that is you Jennifer Fields,
relents the book and permits the book to find
a new owner. All effects invoked through use
of the book will resolve resulting in the book
becoming inaccessible to the Controller forever
more."

The dust radiating from me
dims and disperses.
I don't feel the book's energy.

"Resolved? What does that mean?"

"In Appendix Q,
Subsection Five,
Item B of the book,
the Effect Lifecycle is spelled out clearly."
The Collector chuckles
stopping quickly when its body
touches mine.
"You did read the whole book,
didn't you?"

Guess I'm not the first
one who's been here.
"No…not yet."

"And still you used the book's ability to
your own benefit without knowing the
consequences."
The Collector hisses,
"Tsk, tsk, Jennifer Fields.
That is not being responsible."

Quiet sits between us
for a moment.

Its words sucker punch
my guts as I realize
just how stupid I was.

I read the instructions for our new VCR
but just jumped around in an ancient
magical book about monsters
and demons and magic.

"Resolved means that the effect will be inverted
and returned to the Controller, that's you, and
Subject, whoever benefited from the effect,
three-fold. Resolution can be avoided upon
death and only upon death of either the Subject
or Controller."
The Collector breathes
its swampy damp air
into my ear.

"The good luck, the promotion and raise
would turn into...really bad luck?"
I go limp at the idea.
Dad would be crushed.
He'd probably loose his job
and we'd be out on the street.

"Are you asking for resolution, Controller?"
The Collector asks.

"Do you wish to free the Named?"

I drag in a rasping breath
it catches in my throat.
"That's what most people say."

I can figure out
a way around this.

There is more in the book,
much more for me to learn
to explore
to try.

There's an answer in there
on how to avoid Resolution.

To avoid my family
losing our safety
our good fortune.

"What happens to Joey?"

"His soul will join my collection.
You may bargain for it if you wish
but I would not recommend it until
you finish the book."
The Collector gurgles a laugh.

Whispers

This time I say them.
"Leave her."

And The Collector releases me.

I float up
towards the wire bed frame
passing through the mattress
and stopping an inch above my blankets.

Levitating there for a moment
the purple dust flares from the book
then dims
as I lower to the blankets.

What else didn't I read?

I was so eager to help Dad…
eager to…

Whispers

Yes, that's right,
eager to experiment
eager to know.

Consequences didn't matter.

Could I do it
drowned out
Should I do it.

Is it murder when you can help someone
but don't?

Whispers

Yes, he did sign his name.
He did it to hurt me
and he hasn't been that good kid
for a long time.

He made his choices
and now he has to face
the consequences.

Climbing out of bed,
I open my door.
The hall light is out.
I caress the book
letting my hand linger
on the slick leather cover.

"Thank you."

Whispers

I smile.

Yes, I did what I could.

He signed his name.
He must face the consequences for his actions.

We all do.

Eventually.

Resolution

Dad drops me off at school.

Amy and Audrey
stand at the flagpole.
They're all smiles
and bright pinks today.

I hold my backpack,
my finger tracing the book
through the zipper hole.

Amy's mouth drops
as she sees me.

I look around
for Joey Ruzzo.

No sign.

Going to the flag pole.

"What's your secret Jenny?"
Amy says
tugging her jacket
looking me over.

"What do you mean?"
I clench my backpack
white knuckles
popping like rippling thunder.

"You dieting?"
She sucks in her cheeks
looking skeletal.

"Oh,"
I look to my fingers
seeing the skin strained
taunt, the bones in my elbows
sticking out like pried nails.
"just trying to eat healthy."

"Yeah, healthy."
Audrey motions her fingers down her throat
and fake gags.
Laughing.

"No, it's not that."
I shake away the thought
looking to Joey Ruzzo's
friends.

"Where's Ruzzo?"

"No assholes today."
Audrey sighs
plucking a nail file
from her bag.

Amy giggles.

Joey's friends
wander around lost
talking in quiet tones.

They don't make jokes,
they don't laugh.

Somber faces
sag between them.

Listening carefully
I hear

"I haven't heard from him…"
One says.

"Did he finally run away?"
Another says.

"He wouldn't have left him."
Another says.

All looking
concerned.

All knowing
something
happened.

One catches me listening
and comes over.

"You guys seen Joey?"
He asks
almost pleading.

"No."
Audrey waves him away
with her nail file
not bothering to lift her eyes
to see the panic on his face.
"We don't associate
with things like him."

"Did something happen?"
I ask
pumping curiosity
and concern
into my voice.

The boy nods.

"Joey didn't pick up his brother
this morning."
Tears build up in the boy's eyes.
"He took care of his little brother
cause their parents are shitbags."

I step back.

"Joey'd never missed
picking his brother up."
The damn breaks in one eye
and a tear races down the boy's face.
"Joey was the only thing good in that
kid's life...
the only safe thing...
the only good luck.

Something's happened.
He talked about runnin' but
I didn't think he'd leave his brother
with his parents. Their monsters."

I nod
feeling the salty sting
welling in my eyes.

Slinking away
catching up to Amy and Audrey
as they press through the
crowd near the school doors.

"You act like a jerk
and bad things happen."
Amy mumbles.

Audrey nods.
"Yep."

"Consequences."
I nod.

Whispers.

I squeeze the book
through my backpack.
Yes, he did it to himself.

But…

Whispers.

I nod.

"We all must face the consequences
of our actions
eventually."

I stare into the glass school doors.

Staring at the purple flecks
squirming in and out of my eyes.
They slowly emerge
and drift around my iris
turning brown eyes
radiant purple.

They don't burrow back down.

They stay.

"Yeah…it all catches up with us…"
Squeezing the book,
hearing the whispers.

"Eventually."

Author's Note:

Signature

2020 - 2021

Originally written for my blog, I never published this piece because I thought it was a little too dark. As I prepped the piece for this collection, I rewrote it to make the main character more interesting and have the main character try to save Joey.

Ultimately, this story is about consequences direct and eventual. So many stories circle around what we chose to do to help or hurt others. In this case, Jenny makes a choice not to do anything to save Joey. When it comes down to her family or some kid, she chooses her family and covering up for her past actions.

This theme of powerless kids finding power in books is a recurrent theme in my stories. Perhaps it is the echoes of H.P. Lovecraft or my youthful fascination with "ancient secrets" fueled by Unsolved Mysteries (TV show) and In Search Of... (TV show) but I love the idea of ancient magical books that bring power and knowledge.

If you are a Manga fan and read this, you might see parallels to Death Note. These are not intentional and might have just been Ryuk whispering in my ear.

Do Old Jack and Jenny go to the same school? Is it the same book? Good, and common, questions. Is there a meaning to putting them together in this book? Another good question.

Poor Joey Ruzzo. I wonder if we'll see him again?

IN THE PAINTING

OUCH!
A spark jumps from the doorknob
to my fingers.

I spring back
from it,
not the spark,
the door.

The Boston Art Club's White Door.

Another night,
this night
one year after
my last visit.

He'll be here tonight.

I smell the stench of fish market
Pickman always carried with him
in the end.

Going into the club,
scanning quickly for a crowd
a cluster,
a gasp
telling me
Pickman is here.

But the only crowd
is at the wine bar
with another small cluster
at the hors d'oeuvre table.

Slumping down,
I move around the people
sliding through them
to the first painting,
then the next,
then the next.

All standard Boston Art Club works.

None capturing my soul
to look beyond a cursory glance.

I sip the dry wine
nibble the flat pastries.
Waste words with these "artists"
who have the inspiration
of New York trends and
magazine cover aspirations.

They are not artists.

They are not Pickman.
Where is the bohemian?
Where is the passion?
Where is the…

I look to red wine
swishing around my glass.
The phonies swirling around me
fade.

Swishing my glass
a vortex of ruby pulls me down
to the black crimson.

Pulling a deep drink
feeling the thick
wine
drizzle down my throat,
some leaks from my lips.

I watch it drip
in the window.

The window over the alleyway
where I first met Pickman.
He was coming here.
So was I.

Instant friendship formed.

Reflected in the window
I see a painting
red blotches
pressed out of black waves
a man stands in the center.

Moving to it,
the paint is thick
congealed blobs
smudged not painted.

Parts of the painting are pressed
so deep into the canvas
the threading surfaces.

The red is

intoxicating

but misses the truth.

This is paint.

Pickman didn't use paint
for reds this deep.

"Amateur".
Grunts a man
walking by.
The voice familiar.

Turning
seeing
trench coat,
fedora
wet footprints.

"Pickman?"
I whisper.

I smile.
I follow.

He rounds the corner
to the closed wing
of the club.

I follow
leaving the warm lights
to cool blades of moonlight
cascading across the unfinished brick walls
and splintered wooden floor.

This place was a slaughterhouse
and meat packing factory years ago.

The floor's still stained brown
from those activities
and during hot summer months,
the smells of that work
bubble to the surface.

In the moonlight
the trench coat man
stops at a painting.

I peek around him
unable to see the subject
but seeing

the unmistakable brownish reds
crimson reds,
the copper scent of those reds,
of a Pickman masterpiece.

My spine chills
as I think of our last encounter
the moments after the noises
in his art studio.
The shrieks.

Those inhuman shrieks.

And the photograph
I pulled
from his easel.

His imagined monsters...
not as imagined as I dreamt.
He painted those monsters
those unnatural horrors
from photographs.

"What do you think?"

The man says
revealing the painting.

A Pickman Original without doubt.

The colors,
that red,
the deeper than space blacks,
stormy seas gray.

The subject,
a dark place…this place an alleyway
with one of Pickman's too real creatures
eating something by a dumpster.

Was this scene
from a photograph?
A picture of
daemons from darker places than this
moonlit art club?

He lives with them.
The daemons.
Watches them.
Feeds them.

In return
they feed his
creativity.

Proudly pouring genius
into him.
Greedily guzzling his humanity
in return.

"Do you like it?"
The man asks
removing his hat
showing a face carved in shadow.

"Pickman?"
I ask.

The shadow nods.
He points to the painting.
Red, Pickman's special red,
made of human blood leaks from the frame.

A stream of red
flows to the room's corner
where a huddled form
slurps and snaps splintering bone.

Stepping closer,
seeing it is the contorted creature
from the painting
feasting on a human leg.

The thing is no bigger than a
child but it's face
is mangled by the ill forces
that birthed this accursed wretch
into existence.

Turning away
unable to stomach the inspiration
I see rats racing to the stream.
No, not rats, two legged hairless cats
whose tongues lash out to the bloody liquid
lapping it up
or sucking it through straw like tongues.

Empty gurgling drifts up from them
as the shadowy figure steps towards
the huddled creature.

"Creativity is a hungry beast."
He says with a joyless laugh.
"Isn't it sir?"

I nod.

"Did you hear me?"
I snap awake
still standing in front of the
Pickman imposter painting.

The not quite right red,
the not quite dark enough black.

"I said, isn't it sir?"
The trench coat man stands beside me
his face not in shadow but bathed in light
from the gas lamps.

I don't know him
but I've seen him
at the art club before.

"I'm sorry, what did you say?"
I ask, shivering back to reality.

"Oh, I said, this isn't going
to sell in New York.
That's the point of being here.
Isn't it?"

He scoffs at the painting
sneering at me for making him repeat
his useless words.

I nod
and leave the painting
going to the moonlit
unused space.

It is empty.

No creature.

No Pickman.
But…that felt like him.

It smelled like him.
Old fish market.
Rotten swill water.

Leaving the art club
I head home
wondering if I'll ever
see anything like Pickman's work again.

Horrible.

Terrifying.

But it awoke creativity in me
that I have never found
since he vanished.

"Creativity is a hungry beast…"
I whisper to the night.
"I need to be fed."

Walking home
I hear footsteps
and turn.

No one's there.

My…
dream?
My dream from the art club
tightened my nerves.
Thinking about my last encounter
with Pickman
and the photograph of his model,
put me on edge.

Nothing more.

I keep walking.

Each Tuesday I'll return to the art club
with hope to find him there.
To rediscover the flame he lit in me.

He'll return.
He's an artist and art,
talent,
must be seen.

It cannot sleep silently
waiting to be noticed
or awoken by a kiss.

No. It is ravenous.
His talent will yearn to be seen
and then,
my creativity will be fed.

Stopping at the alley
where we met,
I remember Pickman gathering his canvases.

I carried his portfolio binder
for him and we chatted about the
banality of the Boston Art Club.
A smile comes with the memory.

In the alley
a kid shambles
and drops near a dumpster.

"You okay kid?"
I shout
looking for his parents.

A whine comes from the dumpster.

The kid tripped and got hurt.

I go to him
"Are you okay? Do you need help?"
I ask.

No answer.

Footsteps behind me.
I turn,
no one there.

Looking to the dumpster,
rounding the corner
seeing the kid crouched down
a smell of rotten fish leaks from the dumpster.

A camera flash explodes in the alleyway
throwing long shadows over everything behind me
like lightning.

"Pickman?"

Another flash
shows the kid
is the mangled face creature
from the painting in my dream.

Pickman's next masterpiece.

Another flash
as the alley fills with
two legged hairless cats
flicking their tongues at me.

Another flash
the kid, the monster
glares up at me
ripping me down to it.

Pickman's red
sprays into the air.

Another flash.

Author's Note:

In the Painting

2019 - 2021

At the time of writing, I was listening to Neil Gaiman's Masterclass on writing. He talked about reworking existing pieces. Pickman's Model by H.P. Lovecraft was one of my favorite stories and I thought it was wide open at the end to tell more of the story. The narrator, Pickman's friend, clearly longs for the rebellion and energy of Pickman so it made sense to me that the narrator would just be bored. He's bored and looking for something more.

For this collection, I rewrote the story. The original is still available on my blog, and I hope you enjoy it. Here, I wanted to explore the narrator more and setup a "Return of Pickman".

The narrator in this story is seeking inspiration and realizes how much his creativity was fed from Pickman but ultimately, Pickman is bad for the artist. Most creatives probably have a Pickman in their artistic life. Your Pickman might bring inspiration but beware finding what you were looking for.

While I don't explore the art studio much, the inspiration for the Boston Art Club was an art studio I use to work at in college. One night I was there after dark and the lights went out. It was a bit creepy in total darkness surrounded by strange mask sculptures. In this story, and in Signature, I talk about the slices and blades of light. Those scenes came from the memories of that power outage in the art studio.

Finally, if you are reading the story and saying "hey, cameras didn't have flashes like that in the 1920s" – relax. It is just a story and not historically accurate. To my knowledge, there are not real monsters eating real artists. Suspend disbelief of when instant flashes were available.

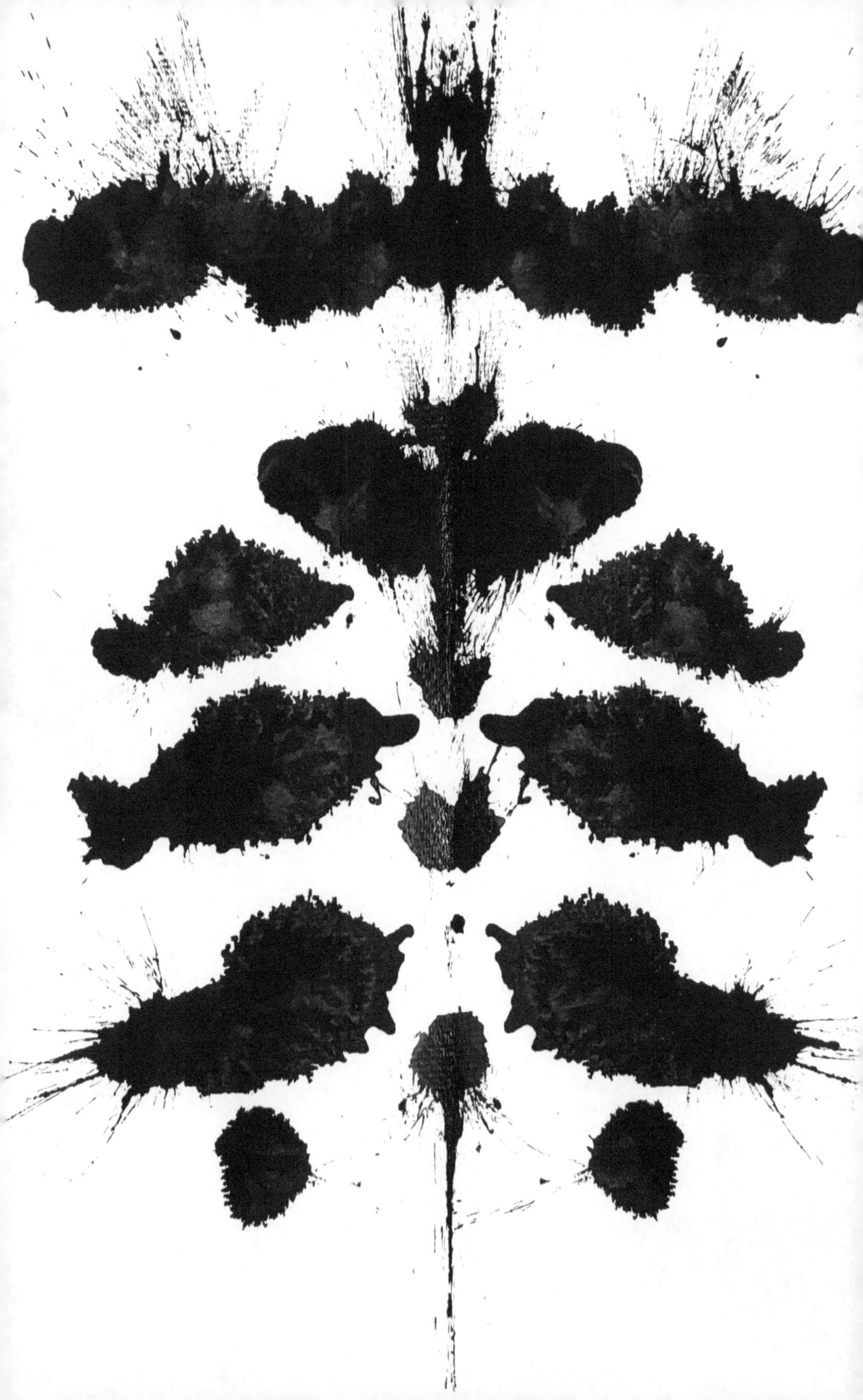

FEAST

I see her in the reflection of my knife. The little girl with wet overalls.

She plays with her friends.

They're all wet. Probably just got out of the river. They laugh and play and enjoy life. I hate her.

I hate that she's happy while my life sucks. Choking my knife, squeezing my hammer, her laughter ricochets in my head.

"Carl, you okay?" I'm brought back to the picnic table. "You hold those any tighter and they'll pop out your hand." Vince smiles nervously as he picks up his next crab and breaks off the legs.

"Yeah, I'm…just thinking." Shaking my head, I put the hammer and knife down. Shame burns in my cheeks. Not for wanting to stab that little girl, I probably wouldn't have done that, but that I'd be seen using a hammer and knife on a blue crab. I'm so focused on being dumped that I can't remember how a Maryland boy should eat crabs. "Thinking about Jess."

"Oh man, you gotta forget her. She's history man." Vince pats my arm leaving streaks of Old Bay on my last clean shirt. "You're not the first guy who caught his girlfriend cheating."

"With my boss." I nod. "Who fired me."

"Yeah, I think you've got a lawsuit there, Carl. Wrongful termination or whatever." Vince snorts a laugh. I shake my head. I know when I'm beat. He took my girlfriend. She took my apartment, all my stuff, and killed the life we could have had.

That little girl's laughing rattles through my head. She's still laughing her shrill and constant trill. Does she breathe? I look over and see her little pigtails dancing around her as she plays duck-duck-goose with the others. Some older people, some younger kids. Must be a family outing. I look around, no one else seems bothered, I guess I'm just being irritable.

Behind the girl's game is another table, a young husband and wife arguing about money problems. Jess and I never argued about money. I just gave her whatever she wanted. She wanted new clothes, no problem. She wanted a new car, here you go. She wanted to go to school for a better job, I gave her my savings and put the student loans in my name. I wish we would have argued more about money. Maybe if I argued more, she wouldn't have left. Wait, she didn't leave. She told me to leave. Is that worse?

"You gonna eat that?" Vince pulls my crab from the newspaper under me. I didn't even get the legs off yet. "This place has the best crabs. They get 'em right from that river there. So, fat! So much meat!" He twists off the legs and claws, popping open the crab shell like a prize box. Vince smiles then digs out the meat and starts licking his fingers, licking the mustard and bits of lungs clinging to his thumbnail. At least he's happy.

I'd like to be happy, but I don't feel anything. I'm not hungry, or sad, or even surprised. I'm not even angry at the laughing girl, I just want her to stop. I just want her to shut up and let me sit, miserable and alone.

Vince holds up a crab, "You ever seen crabs this big?"

I shake my head. How do the crabs get this big? Steroids for crabs? More giggling behind me snaps my attention to little miss pigtails. She's chasing a boy around the circle shouting "I'm gonna get you! Gonna get you again!" The sign above the crab shack catches my eye: Suicide Crabs.

"Why here Vince? You trying to give me an idea or something?" I kick up my lips in a smile but can't hold it. My mask of humor breaks down.

"Nah, things ain't that bad, Carl. You got a lot going for you." He spits crab as he tries to affirm how life is worth living, alone, broke, homeless. "You've got the bachelor life now." I roll my eyes remembering the day Jess and I moved in together and thinking the rest of my life was starting in that moment. Never again sleeping on the floor, with just a mattress and TV. Never again alone.

Tonight, I'll be sleeping on Vince's floor. Sleeping on a mattress that smells like dog piss and puke. This is probably the mattress he passes out on when he's drunk and I'm thankful for it. What else is there? Jess has the apartment. She has our bed. My boss will be sharing it with her tonight. They'll be laughing at me. Laughing at how stupid I am. That I didn't know.

"ALMOST GOT YOU!" the little girl screams.

"DAMN IT!" I shout and turn to the girl. She holds back a laugh like she's going to tell on me. "Just keep it down." I shake my head.

Grabbing another crab, I shift in my seat as Vince stops chewing. He takes a swig of his beer keeping his eyes on me.

"I'm fine." Shaking my head again. He nods slowly, not believing me. I don't believe me either. "I'm going to take a walk. Just want some air that doesn't smell like Old Bay and beer."

"Stay off the bridge." Vince says quietly.

"Ha, ha, ha." I whisper as my eyes slip up to the old bridge straddling the river. The wood is bleached white. Shadows crawl and sway over it from the trees blowing in a chilly breeze. A sigh of exhaustion and dust drifts down from the bridge as a car drives over it. I chuckle in surprise and sigh in commiseration. There's only so much you can hold for so long until you break. Maybe, that was the last car it could take?

Walking past pigtails, she smiles and waves. I want to flip her off. Instead, I try a polite smile but can't find it. Passing the picnic tables with people talking and drinking their beers and cracking their crabs, I remember why I hate crabs. Too much work. Too much talking. I just want to eat in peace. Crabs are a social thing. Jess was social. She was the conversationalist. I just want quiet. You'd think being alone would be perfect for someone like me, but Jess wasn't like being around someone else. She loved to talk to everyone. She made social settings interesting as I followed her around and saw how everyone loved her. I was invisible to everyone but her. Now, I'm just invisible.

"Where you going mister?" A little voice asks.

I look down to see the pigtails girl following me. She giggles quietly, softly, like a lullaby. A sigh slips from me thankful that she's not laughing anymore.

Letting my mind wander, thinking about a life without Jess, I don't notice my feet taking me up the hill.

Down at the picnic table, Vince stares out over the river. He gets up and goes to skip a stone across. He's worried about me. He's a good friend, but I never wanted to be back with him, sleeping on his floor again. I thought that life was over.

"Where you going?" The girl asks again. "Ma said not to talk to strangers, but you look like you need…" she smiles "some guidance." She rocks on her heels with a toothy grin. Her two front teeth are missing like an empty window into her mouth. She tongues the hole, snorting a laugh as she bounces along.

"Just walking." My feet keep moving and I wonder where I'm going. The grass turns to gravel as I get to the road. "You should get back to your mom." I nod to the circle where her family is still playing.

"Ah, none of them are my ma." She shakes her head throwing her pigtails into a hypnotic swirl around her shoulders. Her giggle lowers to a sing song whisper that pulls my attention to her. "I'm just here with some friends." Her voice peps up as her pink bunny slippers rush up in front of me. "It's nice not being alone, isn't it?"

"Where are your shoes?" I look around again and notice we're on the gravel road. Trees lumber over us like sentries watching our procession. The wind rattles their leaves in cheers. I want to wave to them but don't. The little girl skips around me in a circle, bouncing like a sprite, making me nauseous. I look to my feet as gray gravel is replaced by weathered white wood planks.

"Lost them long time ago." She says. A soft giggle bursts out of her and my eyes snap to her again. "You feelin' okay mister? You look real sad. Look like you're all alone-"

"Rough few days." I chuckle but trail off as I realize I want to stop walking but can't. "Where are you going?" I ask, but she just laughs off the question. Her pigtails float around her, waving in the breeze, directing me…forward.

"Following you." She says with a hint a sarcasm. Her sentence could have ended with "silly" or "obviously," but I don't know where I'm going. My mind tries to drift back to Jess but I can't look away from the pigtails. The girl skips along, her arms swinging, her springing steps pulling me after her.

My feet stop on the wooden planks. I'm welcomed by a creaking protest of the wood straining to hold my weight. A boy sits on the railing of the bridge. He was one of the boys from the duck-duck-goose circle.

How'd he beat us here?

Where are we?

The bridge?

I'm in the middle of the bridge looking out to the racing water below and the gray sky hanging heavy on the horizon. The water whispers something too faint to hear. If I got closer to the edge, I might be able to hear.

The girl jumps up to sit on the bridge railing beside the boy. She kicks off her slippers and giggles that melodic giggle. The trees are screaming now, cheering, chanting something…encouragement. "You gonna be okay man?" the boy asks. "You look real sad. Like, you're hopeless."

I shake my head. "What?" Some noise mutes his words like he's talking under water.

"I said, you're hopeless." the boy shouts over the noise. It's getting louder, deafening, droning monotone like something screaming. "You're hopeless. You should jump." The boy hops down and runs towards me. His fingers hook around my wrist. I step back, ripping my arm away and turn to see headlights rushing towards me. The loud noise becomes a horn blaring, screaming at me to move but I can't. This is it. The bridge or the car. This is how it ends. My arm springs up to stop the car. I should have stayed with Vince. I should have stayed with my friend.

The girl laughs. "We need a new friend! Jump!" Her laughter twists into a rapid maniacal heckle echoing over the horn. "Jump! Be OUR friend! Jump!"

THUMP!

THUMP!

The trees jeer.

The girl laughs. Shrill laughter…

Darkness.

***

"Carl?" slap, slap. "Carl!" slap! I put my hands up for defense squinting my eyes to see Vince kneeling over me. Panicked people surround him. A lady in a green sweater is crying, pleading for someone to be okay.

"What Vince what? Stop slapping me!" I sit up as dizziness snatches my strength away.

"Are you okay man? You just got hit by a car." Vince points to the lady in the green sweater. "That lady hit you. You probably can sue her, but she seems pretty nice." He leans closer. "Maybe someone to help you forget about you know who?" A wry smile wraps his face.

"Forget who? The girl? Where's the girl?" I twist around to see where she ran to. My ribs burn with searing screams to stop moving. The woman in the green sweater rushes down to me.

"Lie still. An ambulance is on the way." She says. Her voice is terrified but calming. "I'm so sorry!" Thin fingers wipe tears from her eyes. She smells like lavender. "You just appeared on the bridge. I saw you but couldn't stop in time."

"I'm okay, just dizzy." I sit up again, this time a bit easier.

"Maybe you should get her number, Carl. In case you need to follow up." Vince winks to me. A laugh slips out sending a shiver of pain through me. The first real laugh I've had all week.

"Where are those kids?" I ask.

"Carl, what were you doing up here? I was only kind of joking when I said stay off the bridge." Vince says. "With the week you've had, I don't want you gettin' any ideas on Suicide Bridge."

"Suicide Bridge? You mean, Suicide Crabs?" I ask.

"The crab shack gets its name from this bridge. This is Suicide Bridge. Ghost stories say some kid jumped off this bridge but it's all a story to sell more crabs." Vince says.

"No…" The woman interrupts, "this bridge is closed at night because a bunch of people have jumped off it. Started years ago, with some girl. They found her slippers on the bridge. Body washed up miles down the river."

"Bunny slippers?" The weight of knowing pulls my voice into a crackling whine. The woman nods, confused. I look to where the girl with pigtails kicked off her slippers. They're gone. "Where are those kids?" I grab Vince ripping him down to me. "Those kids that were playing behind me at the table!"

"What kids?" Vince jerks back from me. "You mean that couple you yelled at? They just thought you were an asshole…"

He didn't have to say anything else. I settle back to my elbow, looking at Vince's confusion and then over to the bridge wall. Under us I can hear the rushing water of the river, the inviting whisper fades away drowning in the pungent rot of decaying crab shells.

Off the gravel road I see a pair of pigtails run behind a tree. The girl peeks out, one pink bunny slipper slides around the tree as she winks, grins and dissolves into the darkness.

I can hear her shrill laugh. I can hear her whispering

"Almost got you."

And I wonder how many more she got? How many people she lured to this bridge, to jump, to die here. So many people.

Enough people to keep the crabs fat.

Enough to feed the biggest crabs I've ever seen.

Author's Note:

Feast

2020

I'm not a big fan of eating crabs. I know as a Maryland boy, that isn't a popular thing to say. It's too much work for too little meat and it's social by design. I'm not sure which of those two things I like least about eating crabs.

This story was inspired by a crab shack my mom was telling me about. The crab shack, as my mom says, has huge crabs that are full of meat. She said these crabs would be worth the work. They were good. But it got me thinking about why the crabs were so big.

Combining this question (why the crabs are so big) with a local ghost story, the story of Suicide Bridge, and I had the seed of a story. In the local ghost story, there is a bridge that people jump off to commit suicide and because of that, the bridge is haunted. Where the bridge is exactly is always unknown or possibly not THIS bridge but some other bridge. I thought combining the Suicide Bridge story with the crab shack would answer the question of why the crabs are so fat.

I didn't realize it until reviewing this story that children are often harbingers of peril in my stories. This is funny to me because often I cite children as a great spark that can bring the world to its full optimistic potential. If you pick up on a theme that kids are ill omens in my stories, I think this comes from the idea of innocence gone wrong. That is a common and good horror element that I hope I do service to.

A common question I get is, who are the people with the little girl in the beginning of the story. To be clear, they are the people she has coaxed into suicide on the bridge. She's been busy and if not for the car, Carl would have been the next to play duck-duck-goose.

CAMP CRATER FALLS

"That's not true!"
Donnie snorts a laugh
and looks over the crater's edge.

Water races down
into the blackness
beyond the moonlight.

"Totally true story."
Leon crosses his heart
holding up the scout salute.

"Then where are they?"
Donnie asks.

"Andy's older brother said
you can hear them at night.
Less talking. More listening."

Quiet settles over the crater
over the boys
over their camp site.
Trickling water
rhythmically splashes down
splattering on rocks in the darkness below.

"You can hear their hooves
and squeals."
Leon puts his finger to his mouth
shushing Donnie's next dismissive comment.

"Get closer."
Leon whispers.

Donnie leans to the crater ledge,
chuckling at Leon
listening for anything
past the water.
Looking for anything
past the edge of moonlight glittering
on the falling streams.

"Closer"
Leon leans in beside him,
hulking over him
closing in around Donnie.

Rolling his eyes,
Donnie kneels to listen
focusing into the dark
hearing a faint
clatter of rocks.

"That's the waterfall
hitting some rocks."
Donnie laughs off.

"Just keep listening."
Leon motions to the crater
"They're down there."
Leon puts his hands on Donnie's shoulders
bracing to hear
what Andy's brother said was down there.

Snorts.

Squeals.

Hooves.

"The only thing down there
is a bunch of rocks
and you're 'bility."
Donnie stands up walking away.

Leon leans back,
"What 'bility?"

"Your Gulli-bility."
Donnie busts up laughing.

Shaking his head,
Leon huffs frustration.
He should have seen that coming.

Donnie keeps the fire going
while Leon keeps listening for the
snarls
or snorts
or any sign
of what he knows
is in the crater.

Leon whispers to himself
"The stories must be
at least somewhat
true."

He looks to the empty
camp site.

"That's why no one camps here."

And there's something in the air.
A smell?

A feeling?
An energy?

As midnight approaches
Donnie climbs into his tent.
Leon keeps listening.

"Nothing's down there Leon."
Donnie snatches his sleeping bag over himself.
"I'm going to sleep.
Have fun being creeped out."

"I'm going to sleep out here tonight."
Leon says.

"Suit yourself.
Shout if you get eaten by Pig People."
Donnie zips the tent door.

"They're not Pig People."
Leon quietly grumbles.

Leon doesn't hear anything
as his eyes drift over the moon's face.

No crickets
no chirps
nothing but the still of night,
trickling of water,
and faint scuttling of rocks tripping down
the crater.

He looks over
his eyes adjusting from the moonlight
seeing maybe
a glimpse of movement
outside the campfire light.

He freezes, hearing more rocks falling
from the crater sides
seeing more motion, maybe motion
maybe just tricks of the campfire light.

Flicks of a dying fire
can turn anything into a monster.
A leaf.
A branch.
A rock.

A faint snort crackles through the waterfall
through the popping campfire
coming from Donnie's tent.

Leon looks
seeing the tent shiver
something's inside.

He rushes over
grabbing a stick
unzipping the tent open
to see
Donnie, snorting and squealing
like a pig then busting into laughter
at Leon's panic.

"Not funny Donnie!"
Leon grunts.

"Your face was too much!"
Donnie laughs, pleased with his prank
"Oh no the Pig People are coming!"
Donnie says
mocking Leon.
"Your face!"
Donnie laughs
"Looked like that kid
who peed his pants at lunch!"

Donnie's face locks
into an exaggerated shocked expression.

He chokes trying to breath
through the gut splitting
laughter.

"They're not Pig People!"
Leon grumbles at Donnie.
"Andy's brother said they
had snouts and snorted like pigs."

"Whatever."
Donnie lays back down.

Leon pulls his sleeping bag into the tent
and plops into it.

"Creeped out?"
Donnie asks.
A hint of apology in his voice
but only the slightest hint.

"No. Just keeping my eye on you."
Leon says.
A hint of fear in his voice
perhaps more than a hint.

The two go to sleep
awaking in the morning
packing camp
they head back to town.

Passing the crater's far edge
Leon stops to tie his shoe
noticing beside his foot,
dirt bunched up in a strange
hoof print.

He looks up,
seeing another print
a few feet away.

"Donnie…"
Leon points to the prints.

"Ha, ha. Good one."
Donnie says.
"What'd you set this up last night?
Get me back?"

Leon shakes his head,
slowly stands,
stepping to following the prints.

"Come on Leon.
Leave the jokes to me."
Donnie says
watching Leon go off the trail.

"Stay on the trail Leon."

Leon climbs down
into a ditch
and vanishes
into rustling bushes.

Now it is Donnie's turn
to grumble.

"DONNIE!"
Leon screeches.

Donnie runs
finding Leon in a gully
off the trail
standing beside
a dead deer.

Climbing down,
Donnie chokes back
getting sick
as he sees the deer
isn't just dead
it's dismembered
parts tossed about carelessly
streaks of blood painting the trees.

"What is this?"
Leon gasps.

"It was a deer…
I think."
Donnie pulls on Leon's shoulder
pulling him back to the trail
pulling him away from the corpse.

"Let's just go.
Probably a…"

The bushes
behind the shredded deer
rattle.

Donnie and Leon
step closer to each other
step closer to the trail.

A snort
cracks the rustling bushes
as a gasping squeal
steals their breath.

A ghoulish pale figure
slinks up from the bush.
Its smashed oversized nose points up.
Its eyes are empty slits of black.
Deer parts dangles from its tusks
dripping chunky gore into the bushes
the thing rose from.

Ragged clothes
swing from the emaciated humanish form.
Leon points to the thing's neck
where a Saint Christopher dangles
glinting in the sunlight.

Donnie screams
and the thing runs at Leon
runs through them
goring Leon's hand with its tusks
as it knocks them over
and runs back
to the crater.

More squeals erupt from the crater
a wailing chorus of
hundreds, thousands, of
squealing monsters
drown out the swishing leaves
around Donnie and Leon.

The boys scramble to their feet
shrieking in terror
as they sprint back to town.

Their feet don't stop,
they don't look back,
until they get to town
and double over
gasping to fill lungs
too sore from screaming
to breathe.

They stumble in exhaustion
to the police station
and tumble through the door.

An old officer
rushes to them.

"Boys, what's wrong!?"
The officer shouts.

"Monster."
Donnie gasps
choking on the cold air
seizing his throat.
"Monster. Woods."

"Where? Was it a bear?"
The officer asks.

Both boys shake their head
still struggling to breathe.

"You hurt?"
The officer points to Leon's hand
seeing the slash.

Leon shakes his head.
The stinging pain isn't too bad.
Throbbing, burning,
slithering pain wracking his arm,
but he doesn't want to say it
in front of Donnie.

The boys begin to calm
and find their voices.

They tell the police officer
what happened
and the old officer chuckling,
shakes his head.

"Oh boys. You just got creeped out."
He says.
"Ain't nothing been out there since
old man Hodgeson's house collapsed."

Donnie shakes his head,
"There wasn't any house out there."

"Yeah, that's because it collapsed
into that crater you camped by."
The officer says.
"You boys just got spooked and then
probably saw a wild animal that gotcha
as it ran away."

Leon and Donnie look to each other.
The explanation makes sense.
They were creeped out.
They were listening for the Pig People
and they didn't hear anything all night.

Why would a monster come out
during the day?
That's not a very
monster thing to do.

"You boys are lucky."

"Why?"
Leon asks.

"Lots of people go missing out there."
The officer points to a wall.
"That crater isn't safe.
Collapses like a sink hole
and people who camp out there
go missing."

On the wall
pictures of happy faces
fishermen, campers, hikers,
bold black letters on top of each picture say
MISSING.

"Yeah, it's a nice spot
but accidents happen
and it's too deep to search."
The officer says
shaking his head
shrugging.

One picture
stands out to Leon.

An old man
standing in front of a house.
The photo is in soft sepia tones
older than all the others.

Leon points to the picture,
"Who's that?"

"Oh, that's the first missing person.
Old man Hodgeson."
The officer says.
"Yeah, that old guy was pretty disturbed at the end.
He disappeared a few days before his house collapsed."

Leon walks up to the photo.
Hodgeson holds some tools,
his house behind him.
Probably fixing something.

The police officer laughs,
"Yeah, he saw some animal out there too."
He points to the picture.
"Said, something got him when
he was gardening near the crater."

Leon's eyes focus on the officer's finger.

Donnie chokes on
disbelief
"No…way…"

Donnie sees the scratch
on Hodgeson's hand
a tusk mark just like on Leon's.

But Leon doesn't see that.

He's too busy
looking at the
Saint Christopher necklace
hanging around Hodgeson's throat.

Author's Note:

Camp Crater Falls

2020-2021

This story was based on a writing prompt to extend an existing story. In this case, the story was The House on the Borderlands by William Hope Hodgeson. When I first read this story, I thought of how it would be a good camp story and could be tailored to creep everyone out about the noises in the night.

In the original version of this story, the kids were talking about another group of campers who were attacked by the swine people. I abandoned that story because I wanted to build a story that campers today could tell each other and set a creepy mood. Adding an attack made it too campy (no pun intended) and didn't create a feeling of this could happen in our camp tonight.

There was also a version of this story where Leon pushes Donnie into the crater as bait for the swine people. I didn't like that either because that didn't sound like something Leon would do as I was writing it. The character stepped off the page and said, "Nope". This is a common thing for me in writing. I don't always know what's going to happen. People say "That can't be true you're writing it" but as any writer will tell you, sometimes the characters do things that you didn't expect, and you are just the reporter.

One thing I didn't think about when writing this story: Where are the kids' parents? This struck me as funny in the re-read and I wanted to share it here. I don't have all the answers, but these kids were out camping in this haunted place with a very dangerous drop all by themselves. We'll just go with that.

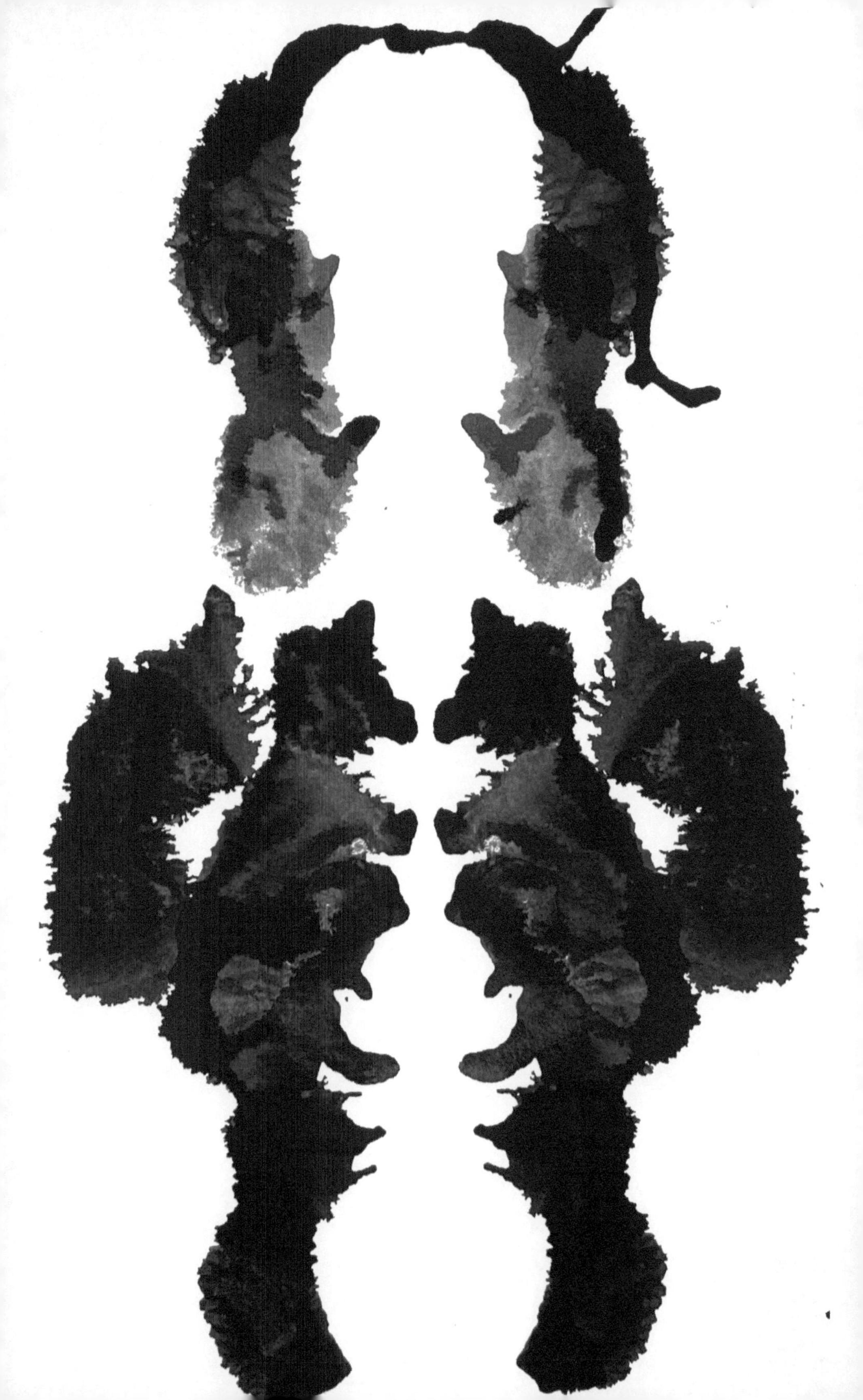

BREADCRUMBS

She left them
where I told her to leave them.

The boy blankly watches
his stepmother
go off into the woods.

The girl blankly watches
the boy
waiting for her cue
to follow their trail back home.

Creaking branches quiet
as the stepmother vanishes
into the woods.

They step to the breadcrumbs
the boy left behind
following it with
vacant faces.

I hurry ahead of them
to get to my house before
they realize their path
isn't leading them home.

The forest
devours the sun
chasing away the day's light
flooding the enchanted forest
with mist and still silence.

Not a snap of twig
nor a rattle of leaves
alerts me to the kids approaching
but the
CRUNCH
of snapping candy from my house tells me

they're here.

They can't resist
a house covered in
treats.

Sweets.

Sugars.

Crunchables
and chewables
all delicious
for things like them.

Greeting them at my door,
I'm sucked into their empty stare
falling through the nothing
behind their eyes.

Those eyes
that aren't theirs.
Stolen eyes.

They lurch forward.
I snap back
breaking free of their
nothingness.

Steeling my mind,
remembering what they are
behind those nothingness eyes,
I smile and
invite them in.

Giving them more candy,
more sweets,
the boy's gaze tracing the treats
the girl's gaze fixed on him.

Then both children look to me.
Their gaze taking in the feast before them.

I smile to them.

Smells of chocolate chip cookies
drift from the oven.
Pleasant sweet smells
covering the sleeping herbs
hidden in the cookies.

Stepping to the oven
I open the door to pull out the cookies
leaning in
to reach them
burning my hand through my thread bear oven mitt.

Snatching out the pan
turning
seeing the children
standing there
a breath away
as I drop the pan
cookies raining to the floor.

They lunge at me.
I dive away.
The boy stumbles into the oven.
The girl pounces onto me.

Snarling,
nothingness eyes,
blistering veins
of desire for

a crunch of bone.

a chew of flesh.

Kicking her back,
kicking her into the oven,
slamming the door,
locking the latch,
as their eyes,
those stolen nothingness eyes
glare out at me.

I watch them in the oven
until their eyes melt
and their flesh falls to ash
to be sure
they
are
dead.

I run through the woods.

Snapping twigs
and crackling leaves
bringing life back to the forest
as I arrive at the stepmother's house.

Knocking.

The stepmother answers
her eyes brighten to see me
as I step in
telling her

"It's done."

The father cries at the table
holding the hands of two children
under their death shroud.

A boy
and
a girl.

"Where did they come from…?"
The stepmother mumbles through tears
of loss,
relief,
and fear.

I look to the children on the table,
seeing the blanket divot
into empty eye sockets.
Where their eyes were stolen from them.
The eyes used to look like children
and stare at me from the oven.

"Demons can take anyone's appearance."
I tell her and point
to the pouch of coin
by the dead girl's leg.

She hands me the pouch.

I snatch it
feeling the weight is about right
for payment.

"Wherever your kids were, those demons found them.
Do you know where they were playing last?"
Stepping towards the door.

"No, they just didn't come home.
Maybe…the caves?"
The stepmother cries.

I nod.
"Sorry you had to deal with this."
I step out the door,
quietly closing it behind me.

Leaving
them to their tears
to their goodbyes
stepping out,
towards the caves.

Pausing,
listening for the silence of those demons.
Fire doesn't always do it.

Depends on the demon.

Listening…
hearing

chirping

snapping

crunching…

CRUNCHing

silence.

Author's Note:

Breadcrumbs

2020

Hansel & Gretel reimagined into a story where the "witch" is a monster hunter, and the kids are the monsters. Yup, kids are the monsters yet again. I hope my kids don't read (too much) into this.

This idea came to me as I was in a "reimagine fairy tales" phase of writing. I love the idea of strong female characters for my daughter to look up to. This is why many of my characters, heroes especially, are female.

The Witch is a common story element in fairy tales. I love inverting the concept that the witch is the villain, or monster, and instead that access to secret knowledge (or magic) makes the witch the only one who can save the family.

Originally posted on my blog, I mentioned a movie that partially inspired this story called "Home Movie". This movie was about a family that ran to a secluded area because their two kids were acting strange. The movie is shot in a found footage style which adds some surprises and creepy realness to the kids' hijinks. I loved the idea of the kids being the unlikely monsters.

Horror movies often inspire me. You can see threads of stories like Event Horizon, In the Mouth of Madness, Nightmare on Elm Street, Midnight Meat Train and Hellraiser throughout the stories in this book. The stories that form in us are a combination of all the experiences and stories that we've gathered. As a movie-lover, I often think of scenes like how I'd visualize them on screen. Building stories on the screen in my mind helps me think through what's going on.

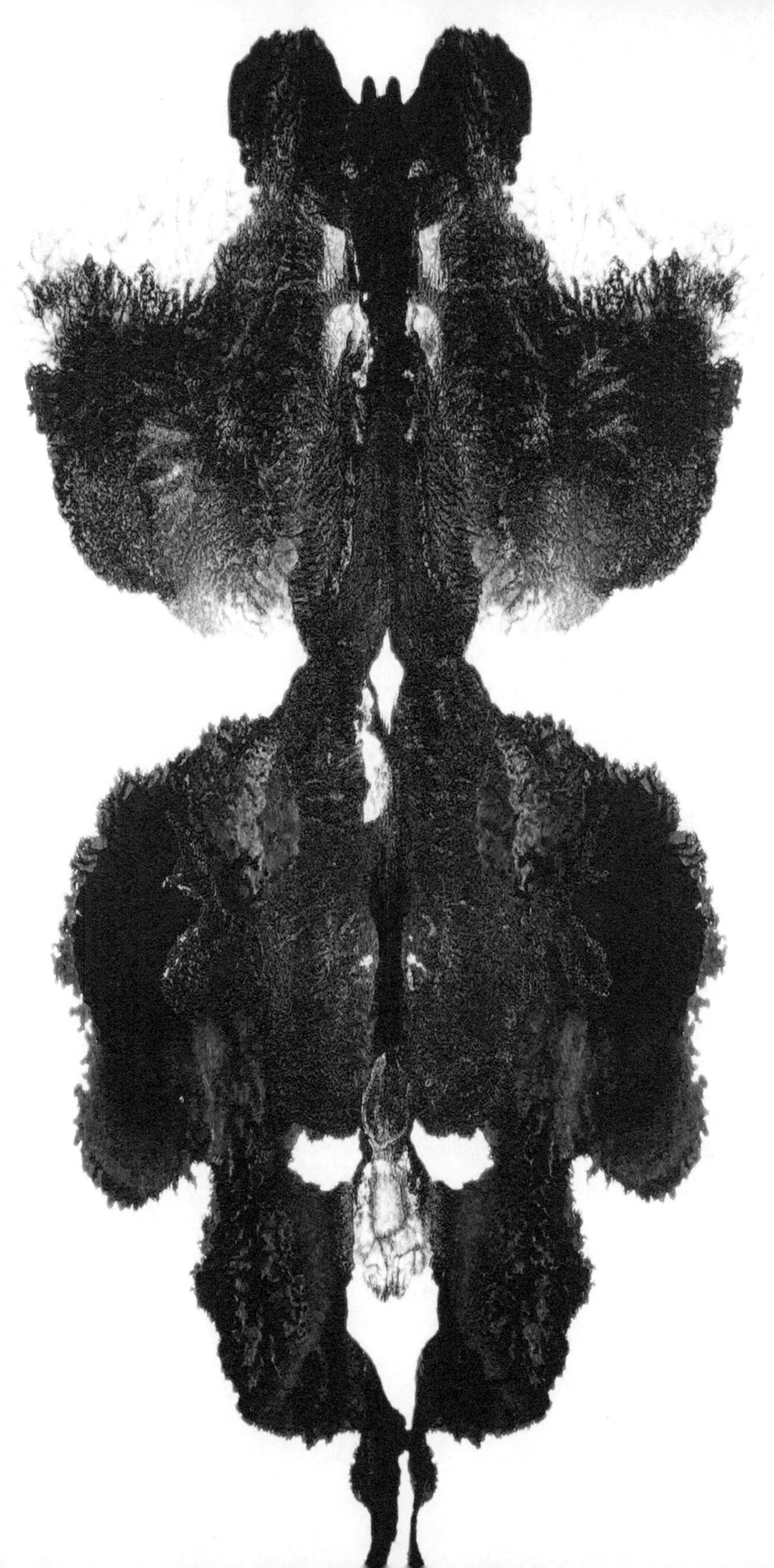

ABBOTS MANOR

"I'm here to see Bernard Davidson's truck."

I press my ID to the camera. The impound lot gate starts clattering open. Wheels squeak and grind into motion revealing neat rows of cars and one beaten, broken blue Ford truck.

While the gate drags open, I get out my private investigator license and the note from my client releasing the truck to me. I can still hear the panic in her voice, how worried she was about her father. She didn't know why his truck was at the impound lot, she hasn't heard from him in days and the police stopped looking for him. I assured her, finding people the police gave up on is my specialty.

The note almost blows out my hand as a breeze rushes over me. I raise my face and enjoy the rarity of country wind rippling over cornstalks. About an hour away from Baltimore, the air is once again fresh and cool. The sounds and smells of the city, carried on hot exhaust and angry voices hasn't yet reached this small-town. But it isn't far. Here, in Glen Coast, the city might be an hour away but the noise, the pollution, are encroaching. Slowly, the city reaches out to towns like Glen Coast to infect them with smog and light and noise.

Baltimore City has been good for me, the people, the art, the social scene but I miss fresh air and starry nights. Nights like I had on my uncle's farm. We'd sit in the field, under the quiet stars and stare at the sky.

The stars I remember clearly but not the quiet. Life in the city has a constant pulse, an omnipresent drone that you can't escape. After being in the city so long, so many years, you forget what real quiet sounds like. Peaceful. Calming. True quiet is a deep breath for your mind to drink in a moment of nothingness and simply relax.

I wonder how many have been driven from the city by that pulse, driven to the country by all the noise. I'm one. I'm ready for some quiet. I drink in the air, a deep draw of cool air just like the farm. Road rage shouts and blaring horns nearby stomp out the memory as the noise devours the possibility of quiet, the possibility of relaxation.

A man wobbles towards me on stumpy legs. He looks like he was smashed by a car compactor. Sucking in a snarl, the man spits thick brown gunk to the dirt. Pointing to the blue truck, he turns and walks towards the only piece of evidence in Bernard Davidson's disappearance.

"You got the paperwork to claim this truck?" his gruff voice rattles with irritation and phlegm.

I hand him the note and flash my license to answer any other questions. He grunts, nods, and waves me to follow.

We walk to the light blue Ford truck. "Is this how it was found?" I ask.

He nods.

"Broken window?" I ask.

He nods again.

Looking through the shattered passenger window, I see a large rock on the floor. Drips of blood splatter the seat and dashboard. The driver window has a spiderweb of cracks spiraling outward from a hole in the center.

In my mind I see the scene, Davidson was driving. A rock flew through his window, hit him in the head. His head hit the driver side window knocking him out.

Ms. Davidson was right to be worried about her father. A truck looking like this and the driver missing for days, smells like foul play.

"Any fingerprints other than Davidson's?" I ask.

The man shrugs. "I don't get paid to be police. Just paid to watch these cars." He grumbles, spits again. His pen scrawls over the release paperwork.

On the driver side I see a mud footprint on the door frame. The pedals are clean. A puddle of blood near the brake pedal has a footprint in it, a footprint matching the one from the door frame. A muddy crust coats the tires telling me he skidded off-road after being hit. Whoever had these muddy shoes came up to the door after the truck stopped, after Davidson was hit with the rock.

"This was in Abbots Manor?" I ask.

The impound guy nods this time with an eye roll. I must be interrupting his very busy day of doing nothing and spitting. He holds out the keys.

Ignoring him, I walk around the back of the truck and see black soot around the exhaust. The muffler rusted and crumbling. Whoever was after Mr. Davidson, must have heard him coming a mile away. This muffler would have woken the dead.

I wave the keys away. "I'll come back for it.". The impound guy grumbles something about wasting his time and I chuckle wondering what else he'd be doing. I go to shut the driver door and notice the muddy footprint only has two toes. My chuckle swells to a laugh as I think about the ninjas on Kung Fu Theater who always wore shoes with two toes. Case solved! Bernard Davidson kidnapped by ninjas. A laugh slips out as I slam the truck door.

***

A quick drive down the highway to a series of increasingly isolated back roads leads to the town of Abbots Manor. At the edge of town, a white sign reads:

Welcome to Abbots Manor, A Quiet Town.

Stopping at the only traffic light in town, I listen to the heartbeat of this place and hear…nothing. No drone of other cars. No clacking shoes rushing across the street. No shouting for taxis or even just people talking. I'm the only car on the road and my car seems quieter here than it was in Baltimore.

I take a deep breath of crisp fall air. A hint of fresh sea water tickles my nose. Taking another breath, I pull in a relaxing gust of quiet that washes away the tension of the city.

The light turns green, and I drive down Main Street. I pass a small grocery store, a hardware store, a family doctor office, all the staples of small-town life. Another deep breath and I can see moving somewhere like here. Relaxing evenings, chatting local gossip at that hardware store, fresh air, friendly people… Looking around I notice, I haven't seen any people. No cars. No pedestrians. No one.

Abbots Manor really is a quiet town.

Pulling up to the police station I laugh to myself at the sign: Voted Best Police Station in Abbots Manor. Voted by who?

I laugh again but quickly silencing as I look around. This place is like a library. You feel guilty making noise and expect some old lady to admonish you for any sound other than a book's creaking spine.

Across the street is a little café called Mama Mazzo's Kountry Kitchen. I bet they have greasy food there. Is there a real Mama Mazzo and does she cook there?

A couple comes out of the café laughing. Finally, I see life here. As their feet hit the steps outside the café, the couple quickly quiets to silent smiles as they walk to their car. They must feel like they're in a library too.

In the police station two officers are on duty. One is diligently doing paperwork; the other is mopping a small holding cell.

"How can we help you, sir?" the officer doing the paperwork says. His attention stays on the paperwork.

"I'm a reporter investigating the Davidson disappearance." I prefer to say 'reporter' to police officers. 'Private investigator' seems to trigger some territorial alpha male attitude. "His daughter told me Abbots Manor was where his truck was found."

Officer Paperwork looks up. "Davidson huh?" He looks me over leaving a loud silence hanging between us. I notice the spectacularly clean police station. The floor shines. The walls are spotless with each desk neatly organized. "Little, you know anything about a Davidson?"

The other officer comes out of the cell. Smiling, pouty lip sticking out. "Can't say I remember that one." He shrugs resting his hand too close to his gun.

"Thank you, officers. I'll just ask around town and see what I can find-"

"Now you mention it…" Officer Paperwork stands up. His steel chair stutters across the tile floor. "I do remember a Davidson. Old man abandoned his truck. Can you believe that Little? He just left his truck sitting there." He walks up to me pressing the air between us into a tense excitement that makes me want to step into him, show him I'm not backing down.

"Sounds…" Little puts his mop against the wall and closes in on me. "Rude."

"Yeah, it does sound rude. Don't you think that's rude Reporter man?" Officer Paperwork steps closer picking up the silence again but this time, the silence has a pulse. A rhythmic whistling as he draws long breathes through his nose. His jaw tenses, teeth grind, each snorting inhale puffing his chest a bit bigger. Around his side, his hand slithers to his gun. My fists clench. He blows out a long, whistling breath through his teeth. "Little, can you check the missing person file and see if we got a police report to help Reporter man?"

Officer Little goes to a rusted file cabinet and pulls it open. Papers erupt out as it screeches open. Is that the missing persons drawer? All the missing people these officers aren't looking for. Little plucks a paper from the cluster and shoves the door closed to a silent shut. No slamming, no clang of metal on metal. Just a quiet muffled resting.

The paper rustles as Little pushes it to me, his other hand still too close to his gun. Snatching the report away, I crumble it to break the pulse of Paperwork's whistling breath, breaking the weaponized silence trying to intimidate me. I turn to leave.

"Mr. Reporter, don't be bothering the people of Roberts Way. They got enough problems without you making noise." Paperwork says as I grab the door to leave. "We'd sure hate to be investigatin' your disappearance." He chuckles. Little snickers. "And thanks for keeping our town a nice quiet place. Have a safe drive out of town now."

I leave chuckling to myself as I pull the door hard to slam it. Thinking of their face as the wooden door snaps the silence around us but it doesn't. Foam padding on the door jamb silences the slam. No matter how hard I pull, it glides softly shut without a sound.

***

In Gabby's, a local pizzeria and bar, I settle in a bar stool to get some dinner and read the shortest police report ever written.

The bartender comes over, gently places a frosted glass of water on a coaster in front of me.

"I'm ready to order." I say.

The bartender nods to the water. "Sorry sir but I think that's all you'll have time for." He points to his watch. "Going to be getting dark soon and you'll want to be getting home."

I look at the water. A drip drags down the side.

"It's good water sir. Not trying to be rude but we don't have lodging. And deer are all over these roads at night. It's not safe driving. You oughta get on home soon."

Nodding, I thank him for the warning and sip the water. It is delicious water… crisp, fresh. Not bottled or purified, probably right from some stream here in town. He walks away leaving me to the police report.

Details of Event: Citizens at the corner of Roberts Way and Thoth Avenue filed a noise complaint against Mr. Bernard Davidson on October 25th at 7pm. Officer Little and Officer Moore responded finding Davidson's abandoned truck. Mr. Davidson's truck was breaking the local noise ordinance with his loud exhaust.

Actions Taken: Officers notified county to come pick up the truck for impounding.

I read it again, and again to see if there is something I'm missing. My water is empty, has been for a while. I guess no refills here.

An eruption of laughter startles me. Jumping to grab my gun, remembering those days are over. I calm seeing the corner of the restaurant where a group of moms are having a lady's night. They laugh and hoot and holler shouting something to the bartender about some lady named Amy. I wonder who Amy is.

This is the bar scene of the country. Drunk people yelling. They're having fun, they're enjoying life. They must be out of towners. They missed the sign: Abbots Manor, A Quiet Town.

My eyes drift to the bartender to see his response. He nods and laughs to himself. The women laugh again, this time quieter. Perhaps they aren't as loud as I think. Maybe it was like the frogs on my uncle's farm. When they croaked it was always so loud and when they stopped, the night was quieter than it ever had been. I return to the police report.

The officers must have seen the blood in the truck. They must have seen the broken windows and rock. And with a muddy footprint on the door frame there must have been footprints around the truck. I think back to Ms. Davidson's request, when she asked me to find her father.

She said, "He was no angel. He had a dark side with the drink. He used to run with a rough crowd, and I'm worried his past caught up to him. I think something happened to him. I knew there was something wrong when he missed his Masons meeting last night. He always wears his Mason ring and wouldn't miss a meeting unless…"

The lady's night crowd start to gather their things and head to the door. One of the women slurs something to the bartender about Amy again as they all laugh red faced and teary eyed. As the door opens, their faces turn to stone. Laughing stops. They nod to each other as they walk to their cars. The one woman, the woman yelling about Amy in the bar gets into a blue hatchback. Her friends all find their car. Officer Paperwork should be breathalyzing people stumbling out this door.

Checking my phone, I see it is 5pm. The women drive off as the sun slips down the horizon into a purple haze of dusk.

Mr. Davidson's truck was found on Roberts Way and Thoth Avenue. I leave Gabby's to find that intersection. To see where he disappeared. My gut tells me that corner is the scene of a crime.

How could the cops leave this? They are supposed to serve and protect the community not let people disappear. Not ignore a crime scene?

"Some bodies are better left not found." My old chief said. That's never true. As police we always had to move on. Now, I can focus, I can help people figure out what happened. Find their loved ones.

No more, "Sorry ma'am but I'm on another assignment now." Seeing the crying faces of family members when you say you're giving up. When those cops gave up on my uncle. Mr. Davidson isn't lost. He was taken from his truck. And I'm going to find him. I always find them. I don't let it go for someone else.

As I step out of Gabby's, I notice the thick foam between the door and the wall. Looking again at the walls, the foam covers the place under posters and maps of Italy. Sound proofing foam? The townsfolk really mean it when they say: A Quiet Town.

***

The corner of Thoth Avenue and Roberts Way is the edge of town. A flickering streetlight signals the beginning of Roberts Way. This dim light is the last light of Abbots Manor. All civilization stops here. Beyond this road are places too dark to see.

Looking back to Abbots Manor, seeing dim streetlights marking the way back to Main Street I recognize the darkness of a country night. I had forgotten just how dark the world can be outside the city, outside the haze of lights and noise that seem everywhere. Here, the world is empty.

On one side of Roberts Way, faint golden light leaks from windows of picturesque homes. Each brick house is a copy of the next with metal gates separating small yards from the road. Each gate has foam stoppers like the police station door.

These houses look like a photograph of the American Dream. They represent the good life promised by sitcoms and TV commercials since I was a kid. I could imagine living here, maybe get married and start a family. Kids playing in the yard, maybe chasing a dog, counting stars every night. Looking up, seeing the stars again my eyes drift to the other side of Roberts Way.

With no moon, the field is featureless until slowly my eyes adjust, and a hill of dead grass emerges from the shadows. Gray grass that flaps in an early winter wind like fingers reaching from shallow graves. With each moment those fingers claw through the darkness revealing more field leading to a gray stone house on the hilltop.

Encircling the house is what was once a white porch. The posts are cracked and collapsed like broken teeth jutting from a malformed mouth. Black windows are empty eyes staring with jealous rage at the homes of Roberts Way. A faded red door hangs from one hinge on the door frame. On the second floor, a broken white balcony dangles from a cracked glass door.

I imagine once upon a time that glass door looked out over the entire town of Abbots Manor. Now, it looks to the faint golden windows of Roberts Way with a hungry longing for what? The light? The laughter of families inside? Perhaps it longs for a time before the town crept to the edge of the dead grass?

On the asphalt of Roberts Way, black streaks, tire marks lead into the dead field. Mud is gouged into tire tracks where Davidson's truck skidded towards the house on the hill. Broken glass sparkles from the road where the rock hit the window. Feeling the frozen mud tracks, I follow them to where they stop. Mounds of mud shows where the tires sank too deep. Divots show Davidson tried to rock the truck out. Probably trying to escape.

Around the mud gouges are footprints. Footprints on the passenger side. They, whoever it was, came from the passenger side and pulled him out. Footsteps lead back towards Roberts Way along with a flat streak in the mud. Flat like someone dragging a body.

Following the streak, I see the mud tracks cross Roberts Way and lead to one of the metal gates. Beyond the gate the muddy streak continues towards a set of cellar doors. The gate's hinge is broken. Davidson must have kicked it while being pulled to that basement.

"Gotcha" I whisper.

Headlights blind me as a car pulls up to this gate. The driver flicks off their lights and my eyes adjust to see the blue hatchback from Gabby's.

The loud drunk lady who screamed about Amy quietly steps out of the car. She carefully closes her door then gasps and startles when she sees me. Her hand instantly claps over her mouth as her eyes bulge in horror. Still clasping her mouth, she shakes her head slowly, sweat beading on her forehead at the sight of me standing at her gate. She knows, she's been caught.

"Excuse-" I start and instantly stop seeing her violent horrified face.

Tears drag mascara down her cheeks. A pleading whisper slips through her hand. "Shhhh!!!"

Her eyes jut from me to the stone house then to the brick houses on Roberts Way. Those eyes are bloodshot and ready to burst with panic. "Shhh…" She whimpers.

I step back. Her fear is contagious as a flood of anxiety engulfs me but why? Why am I afraid? She's the one who's been caught. But, caught doing what? Caught sneaking home from the bar? Caught dragging a body into her basement?

Caught in some other small-town secret?

"Sorry…" I whisper. "Do you live here?" I ask trying to calm her.

She shakes her head feverishly patting her hands down, signaling to be quiet. "Shhhh!" She grabs the gate, opens it, and rushes in. "You gotta get out of here." Her voice is as soft as a breath. "Don't wake it up." She breathes again as she rushes off to her house.

I grab the gate and pull it to follow but its locked. Pulling hard, the gate releases a muffled rattle. The noise drifts into the night with a faint garbled cat's cry responding.

My spine shivers. My guts drop into a pit at that sound. I snap around to the stone house, that's where the noise came from. My face meets a frozen gust of wind, chilling, taking the breath from me. The windows of the stone house are scowling at me, admonishing me for making the faintest noise.

Shaking my head and looking again…it is just an old house. The cat, or whatever animal that was, must be in the house.

Silence comes back thicker than before the cat's cry. Was there any noise before? No chirping crickets. No buzzing lights. No white noise of families, no kids playing, no parents talking about the stars in the yards or houses.

I stare into the empty eyeless anger of that stone house. I've never felt silence this oppressive. Not a forced silence, not an intimidating silence but the absence of resonance. I can feel, the stone house devouring the sounds around us. Sitting up there on the hill, that house sucks in noise and light and exhales the frost-bitten chill of winter wind. That house isn't just quiet and dark, it is a void of emptiness that invites you to look deeper, listen harder, to find whatever might be lurking inside.

Crunching gravel breaks the silence. A dark car pulls up beside mine at the end of Roberts Way.

The flickering streetlight casts long shadows over Officer Paperwork's face. He pulls out his club and puts his finger to his lips hissing a faint "Shhhh" that carries over the frigid breeze. Officer Little walks up the other end of Roberts Way. They close in quietly, slowly and I grab the metal gates, shaking them to get in.

None open.

I want to scream for help but then see the mud divots from Davidson's truck and realize, no one will help me here. The golden glow from the houses darkens as people stare down at me from their windows. Citizens of Roberts Way watch as the officers prepare another missing person case. I go the only direction I can, into the dead field, towards the stone house.

I stumble over the mud divots hitting the frozen ground with a stinging grunt. The cat howls again and the officers hiss their admonishment to be quiet. As I roll over, I see the two officers pacing only a few feet away along the edge of Roberts Way like tigers prowling their cages. They don't step on the gray grass.

Their eyes jut from me to the house behind me. I push against the mud to stand,

and I see a two toed footprint. Standing where the driver's side of the truck would have been, there is a two toed footprint in the mud leading to the stone house. Closer to the house, something sticks out of the mud. Something flapping in the wind. The two toed footsteps lead to it.

A closer look at the footprint shows it isn't a ninja shoe but a malformed foot. The toes are webbed…or melted together and the heel points like a talon. The weight of the step is deeper in the center of the foot and not rolling heel to toe like a person but stomping into the mud like stilts.

I crawl over to the flapping thing and pull it out the mud. It's a photograph. A photograph of Bernard Davidson naked, throat slit, arms severed in some basement probably the basement of the lady with the blue hatchback. All his parts are gathered in a clear plastic storage bin. Written on the photo with black marker: "We took care of it. He's in the truck."

Another photo sticks out of the mud closer to the house. It rips as I pull it from the mud, raising another garbled whine from the cat in the house. The cat must be hurt or in heat. Maybe that isn't a cat?

Looking back, the officers stand down the hill on Roberts Way, watching me. This photograph is another one of Davidson, naked, dead, horrified in his contorted expression.

The two toed prints continue to the house, and I see another photograph on the mangled mouth of a porch.

Before I know it, I'm at the red door. The corner of another photograph is sticking out the door showing Davidson's face screaming, I imagine him pleading for the torment to stop. His throat isn't cut yet in this photograph. What happened to him? Who wanted these photos? What was taken care of?

I grab the door handle stopping as I see around the door, the stone work's grout has crumbled to decay like the over used veins of a junky. The door might rip right from the wall sending all the stones of this house crashing on me almost as heavy as the weight of this dark silence.

I activate the flashlight on my phone, but it flickers out leaving me in deeper darkness than before. My battery is dead. I thought it was charged…? It was charged. I know it. I don't make rookie mistakes like that.

Pulling on the door handle the hinges roar a squealing protest. Behind me a gasp blows out from Roberts Way. I turn, seeing the officers are now joined by the families of Roberts Way all watching me go through the red door into the stone house. They slowly rub at their temples and shake their heads. I can't see their faces, only their empty silhouettes in the last streetlight of Abbots Manor.

The police stand with the town. Were they serving and protecting? Was I making the noise they warned me about?

A faint blue mist slithers through the house cresting over blanket covered furniture and splintered wood flooring. A sour wind blows through the windows making the curtains whip about like tentacles striving to catch a meal.

Another cat cry, or was that a baby's cry? Was that the waking whine of a child made twisted and shrill by this frigid wind?

The muddy footprints lead upstairs and another picture dangles on the edge of the landing. I step on the stair and look up, pausing, thankful the noise is upstairs and not down. Thankful that I don't have to descend into some subterranean torture chamber to find out what happened to Davidson, to tell his daughter what happened, to find whoever has these pictures. I can't let Mr. Davidson go. His daughter needs answers. She needs closure.

The crying comes from upstairs. It churns my guts pulling on some primal warning. Stop it. It's just a cat. An injured cat or some animal. Nothing more.

Stepping on the first stair I pause expecting the creaking of wood. I hear nothing and silently continue up the stairs.

On the landing, I see the hallway stretches to a closed door. That's the room with the balcony. That must be where someone, sometime long ago looked out over Abbots Manor. I wonder if they marveled at the growth of the town or abhorred the idea of people edging towards this house. The townsfolk creeping towards that window like an infestation slithering closer with each new house, each new road. The muddy footprints lead to that last door. Other doors flank the hallway leading to other rooms.

I follow the footprints. Stopping at one door where the gentle gliding of a white rocking chair catches my eye. A crib sits beside the rocking chair. A bundle of blankets mounded in the center under a broken and drooping mobile that sags into the crib. Animals like giraffes and elephants dangle from the mobile like a noose waiting for a neck.

The wind must have blown the rocking chair.

Looking to the chair, the rocking continues but there is no wind. The room is still with only the chair moving. In the chair, another photograph of Bernard Davidson is held up by a shadowy hand. Someone in the chair is looking at the photograph.

"Hello-" I say.

The whine starts again. Yes, it is a baby. A baby's waking whine but crackling and lingering like the song of breaking glass. The sound hangs in the air, sculpting a dread like shattering basement windows when you're home alone.

Quiet tension engulfs the room.

Then a cry bleeds through gurgling sounds as if the child were drowning. Inside the crib, the mound of blankets shift in a jerky whipping motion. The rocking chair stops, the photo is lowered to their lap.

I suck in a deep breath as everything in me tenses. My eyes strain to see the blankets. My fingers stretch to find anything, anything I can grab. The bundle twists again, twists like a writhing worm… The shadowy hand drifts over the crib and taps the mobile sending it slowly, silently, turning. The elephants and giraffes stutter into motion with a faint rusty grind. Dust drifts down into the crib like toxic snow coating the blankets.

Another whipping twist as the baby reaches to the mobile. The filth crusted blanket slips back revealing a wisp of formless shadow stretching to the mobile. The convulsing blankets settle. The waking child quiets again. Drips of hissing coos carry the horrible thing back to sleep.

The chair starts rocking again, the photograph lifted again. I didn't realize I stepped into the room. I didn't realize I walked up to the rocking chair moving around it to see who had the muddy feet, to see who had the photograph.

Waves of revulsion hit me, pushing me back. My eyes water to blur out what's in front of me. A crushing silence rips away a scream that must escape. No breath, no sound, just staggering away from…from it.

A person didn't sit in the chair. It was a rippling shadow with stars inside it. Pin pricks of light warbled and pulsed with my gasping breath. Its body ripples in time with my shivering flesh. My eyes fall to the two toed, taloned feet.

My teeth grind as my mind screams to pull away, to look away but I can't. I can't spare myself the misery of seeing that eye. That single eye swirling like a spiral galaxy in the infinity of the thing's being. That eye fixes on me sending a fleet of spiders crawling through my mind. Those spiders dig through my thoughts with hot poker pinchers tingling, clicking, whispering.

"He woke the baby." The thing in the chair holds up the picture in shadowy formless wisps. It doesn't talk…it puts the thoughts in my head as if I thought those words.

Rubbing my temples, trying to press the thoughts out of me. I stagger back. Tripping over something as the voice comes to me again.

"Don't wake the baby. She needs her rest. Feeding is such hard work."

I hit the ground finding the thing I tripped over was the gnawed remains of an arm. An arm with a Mason ring. Bernard's arm…

"Shhhhh…"

My breath is ripped away by the void of this place. The stone house dissolves into darkness. I drift into the silence of unconsciousness.

***

Orange sunrise fills my car as I wake up on the corner of Roberts Way. A photograph of Bernard Davidson sits on my lap and as I pick it up, his Masonic ring on my finger glittering in the sunlight. The picture falls to the floor as I quietly start my car, turn around and go to the police station.

Walking into the station, Officer Paperwork and Little lean against the wall watching me curiously. I place the picture and the ring on Paperwork's desk.

"Please make sure that ring gets to Davidson's daughter."

As I turn to leave, Officer Paperwork clears his throat and says "We had to take care of it. He was going to wake it."

"I know." I say without stopping. "But everyone deserves closure."

Ensuring the door closes quietly behind me I hear footsteps across the street. A couple walks into Mama Mazzo's Kountry Kitchen, laughing as the door closes behind them.

I drive down Main Street and out of Abbots Manor. My speed grows faster and faster after each backroad until I hit the highway. I race to my apartment in Baltimore City.

My feet pound up the stairs. I slam the door unleashing echoes of metal on metal filling my foyer. Quickly bolting the lock, I pause to drink in the loud clack of the bolt sliding into place. A dog barks in response to my clacks, slams and pounding feet. Sirens swirl in the streets around me and I sink into my couch with a loud sigh. A sigh that mutates into the scream that I couldn't let escape in Abbots Manor.

I turn on the TV pushing the volume up to the max. My neighbors bang on their walls. I laugh loud cackles. Rocking on my couch I laugh feeling a tingling in my mind as something listens to all the noise enveloping me. The tingling flees as I rub my temples, pushing it away and scream louder, loud enough to be all I can hear.

I run to my balcony and listen to Baltimore. People shout, horns blare, buses roar, all building the chorus of the city keeping the oppressing silence and things that dwell in it where they belong…on streets like Roberts Way, in towns like Abbots Manor.

Author's Note:

Abbots Manor

2020

When I was a kid, there was a local ghost story about a man whose truck was too loud. One night, the man was stopped, ripped out of his truck and murdered. Why? Because his truck was too loud. Note, this was just a ghost story as far as I knew but as kids, we believed it as gospel.

Ghost stories are supposed to have a moral or something for the listener to reflect on. In this case, the moral was: be quiet in a quiet town. Our main character here is learning that lesson. He wants quiet until he experiences the quiet of a small-town gripped in fear of what lies at the city limits.

The house at the edge of town also represents a place where civilization slowly creeps to your doorstep. I find this a fascinating concept as many civilizations throughout history have watches the march of invaders coming to their doors. As people spread throughout the world and cultivate the few wild places that remain, I imagine what is watching us creep closer. Does the thing watching welcome us or smile to itself and see snacks?

The citizens of Abbots Manor are not villains and are not being cruel. They just want to live in peace. I tried to strike a balance between the character feeling like the town is against him and making the townsfolk relatable.

Abbots Manor is inspired by a real place (not called Abbots Manor). Some of the ghost stories of this place formed my passion for hauntings and monsters. The old house in Abbots Manor was once a real house but it was torn down for a new housing development a few years back. I've considered writing a sequel to Abbots Manor to explore where the creature of the house goes now that its home was taken. But I haven't gotten there yet.

CLOSING NOTES

BLOTS are not globs of ink. They are drips on a broader canvas. The people, places and books in these stories follow me around from story to story. You probably noticed links. If you did not, I'd encourage you take another read.

Was that the same Donnie in Camp Crater Falls and Old Jack?

Could the artists in our stories have encountered each other at some point?

Could a quiet town have a seaside festival?

Sometimes I find Old Jack sitting at a table or the resident of Abbot's Manor rocking in a dark room. Stumbling on these people (and things) are part of the joy of writing. A surprise to me when it happens and a pleasant surprise when a story comes with them. In REFLECTIONS, Bernard says that when ghosts talk we should listen. For me, when these characters talk, I've learned to listen. While I'm not always a GOOD listener, I love to write what they tell me.

I hope you enjoyed reading BLOTS as much as I did writing it.

Thank you for spending time with my stories,

Tim Kulp

BLOTS 2014 - 2021

Other Stories from

T. Kulp & Cy Borgmyn

[dis]connection by T. Kulp

BLOTS by T. Kulp

Monsters Dance to Twilight by Cy Borgmyn

The Light of Enki by Cy Borgmyn

Coming Soon

The Trial of Mirror Mountain by Cy Borgmyn

Library of Lessons & Lies by T. Kulp

[un]learn by T. Kulp